FINALLY
RiffRaff Records – Book 9

L.P. Maxa

ALSO BY L.P. MAXA

RiffRaff Records
Royalty
Legacy
Infamy
Loyalty
Sanctuary
Piracy
Certainty
Inevitably

The Devil's Share
Play Nice
Play Dirty
Play Fair
Play Softly
Play Hard
Play For Keeps

St. Leasing
Mouth Watering
Breath Taking
Jaw Dropping
Heart Stopping
Soul Crushing

Other Novels
Happy Place
Stumbled into Love
Rescued

www.**BOROUGHSPUBLISHINGGROUP**.com

FINALLY

ISBN: 978-1-951054-7

To everyone who stuck with these characters,
devouring all sixteen of their love stories

ACKNOWLEDGMENTS

This time, first and foremost, I need to thank my editor, Michelle. These two were a struggle for me, and I don't know if I would have had the strength, or brainpower, to get their story written without you. And, of course, my husband and daughter, their patience with me and my process is unparalleled. Thank you to Amy S. for listening to me complain. Thank you to my mom for reading every attempt. Thank you to Amy H. for always keeping me up to date and making sure I exist in the romance writer world. Thank you to my baby sister who basically told me to shut up because I was ruining the book she was waiting for. You reminded me that people love Crue and Avory, and that they deserved the best. And last, my Smitten Kittens, you guys are a constant well of support and laughter.

AUTHOR'S NOTE

Writing Crue and Avory wasn't easy. They were the last story to tell, signaling the end of my time with The Devil's Share, RiffRaff Records, and The Devil's Spawn. *Play Nice* was the first book I had published with Borough's Publishing Group, and I couldn't have predicted that those four rockers would spawn another generation of characters for me. I love Dash, Smith, Jacks, and Luke. But the love I have for their kids? It's hard to put into words without starting to cry. I know it's sad that this series is done, but please know these characters live on in my mind. They're happy, and they're all still in love. They go to Friday Family Dinner and their children play together, running wild through the compound. I am eternally grateful for this experience, for these love stories I got to share with the world.

Thank you for reading. Thank you for loving these people as much as I do.

LP

FINALLY

Words can't say what love can do.
~Bon Jovi

Prologue

Crue

I didn't come out of the womb in love with Avory Connor. It wasn't a soul connection that started from the first moment our hands touched. No. I'm sure the first time I touched Avory it was to pull her hair or some shit. In all fairness, the last time she let me touch her I was probably pulling her hair…but that was years ago. I fucked up, and she still hasn't forgiven me. It didn't matter that I did what I did to spare her, and to spare my twin. It didn't matter that I groveled at her feet, it didn't matter that I'd gotten down on my knees and begged her to take me back. That girl held a grudge like no other.

I digress.

What I'm trying to say is this is a love story. Avory's and my story. It isn't as pretty as the rest. It isn't all tied together in a perfect package with one of those glittery bows on top. It's messy. It's sad, and it's twisted. But it's ours. And I wouldn't trade one moment of fighting with her for ten thousand moments of happy with someone else.

It took me over a decade to realize that Avory was the girl for me. It took me a couple years to lose her. And it looks like it's going to take me an eternity to win her back.

Chapter One

Avory

Then

Crue had been acting weird all weekend, ever since that whore came up to us at Benson's party. She wanted a date with him in exchange for not spreading stupid rumors. He was probably freaked at the prospect of our parents finding out that we were together, which we had been for like two years or something, since I had been a few weeks shy of my sixteenth birthday when we started seeing each other. But we were in love, and I was almost eighteen now. Even if my dad lost his shit, we'd only have to deal with the repercussions for one more school year. And I could even try to graduate early. I had the grades, even though most people assumed I was an airhead cheerleader.

I watched as Cash held tight to Katie, talking to his mom and smiling like the world was his for the taking. I was happy for Cash and Katie, but I was almost a little jealous. I longed for the day that Crue and I didn't have to hide the way we felt about each other. Our love story was different from Halen and Beau's, even though we were two Devil's Spawn raised as family who fell for each other late one night on our parents' land. And Cash? Well, he'd been our biggest supporter, so I needed to step up and do the same for him.

I made my way through the crowd, coming to stand with my Aunt Lo, smiling when she invited me to dinner. Katie was leaving soon, and Cash was going to Europe with her for the rest of the summer. Of course I'd be at dinner. I wouldn't miss it. Cash was one of my best friends, and I'd miss him like crazy while he and Katie were seeing the other side of the world together.

"Hey, can I talk to you for a second?" Crue grabbed my arm, speaking to me for the first time since we'd all met up for breakfast. His tight grip sent chills and relief flooding my anxious system. When he was with me, I could breathe. He was possessive and demanding, and he was rough. But I craved every damn second of being loved by Crue Matthews.

"Crue, don't manhandle her like that." His mom slapped his hand. "What's wrong with you?"

Ha. If she only knew how much I enjoyed it when her son *manhandled* me. I stepped away, fully okay with letting Crue pull me into the nearest empty bedroom to "talk." We'd spent more time apart the last couple of days than we had since we started dating, and I was yearning for him.

"Uh, Luke, which one of your twins is in this picture our publicist sent over?" Uncle Smith's irritated tone rose over the noise, making everyone quiet down.

All eyes went to Crue and me. Well, all eyes that knew we were together. There was a pic of Crue and me? Had someone followed us? No, that couldn't be right, we were so careful. It was probably a picture of Cash pretending to be Crue. He probably broke down and agreed to go on that date in Crue's place. But wait, why would there be a picture? Cash wouldn't do that to Katie. He was in love with her. I put my hand to my stomach, the sudden urge to vomit crawling up my throat.

"Okay. Well. Since there is a topless girl, who thank god *isn't* Katie, I'm assuming it's Crue." Uncle Luke's gaze shot across the patio, his eyebrows raised in annoyed disbelief.

"No." I didn't mean to speak out loud. I didn't mean to throw Cash under the bus. But like, I also couldn't handle them insinuating that Crue was screwing someone else. I felt like I was going to puke any second, my guts churning and twisting. "It's Cash, right?" I pulled my hand from Crue's ever-tightening grip as a chill went down my spine. "You had a date last night, didn't you?"

Katie backed away from us, shaking her head. She was speaking but I couldn't seem to hear her over the ringing in my ears. I felt like I was witnessing a car crash and I couldn't look away. Either Katie's heart was about to be shattered or mine was. I put my hand to my chest, trying to hold in my fear, my hope, my disappointment, and my utter shock.

"I hooked up with some random girl last night, who the hell cares? It's not like it's something new or anything." Crue stepped closer to me, holding my wrist behind my back, stroking his thumb over my rapidly beating pulse. He was trying to keep me calm, trying to keep me connected to him. "Obviously I should have had her sign an NDA, but hindsight's twenty-twenty. She's over eighteen, the whole thing will blow over in a few days."

I couldn't believe what I was hearing. I pulled away from him, and with the loss of that contact, I severed everything that was between us.

Crue'd hooked up with that bitch from school. He'd cheated on me. He'd destroyed us, and there was now photographic evidence plastered all over the place. There were pictures of the exact moment the love of my life had smashed my heart.

How was this happening? How was this my life? In that moment, Crue lost me, and lost my trust. He'd ruined everything that we had, everything that we *would* have.

He threw it all away.

And I felt like I was fucking dying.

Chapter Two

Crue

Then

Avory wouldn't speak to me. It'd been five days. I tried calling her. I tried texting. I tried crawling into her window, and found it locked for the first time in our whole fucking lives. Her shades were drawn, her curtains closed. And I deserved every single drop of her red-hot anger.

I'd gone on the date with every intention of leaving as soon as I could, of coming home to my girl. I was going to tell her, I was going to explain that I'd done it for her, for Cash. I was buying us time, time to get off this compound together, time for her to turn eighteen. I didn't see the harm in going to one dinner. It was a few hours of bullshit I had to endure to enjoy a lifetime with Avory. But then that chick had asked me to pull over, asked if we could sit on the side of the road for a bit so her parents would think we were out hooking up. She was hell-bent on pissing off her mom and dad. She wanted them to know she wasn't theirs to command and she demanded my help. Not inclined to oblige, I'd left her in the cab of my truck and had gone to smoke a joint on the tailgate. It was still early. I'd intended to pick up Avory as soon as I got home. She was having girl's night anyway.

But then the bitch followed me, climbed in my lap, and took off her shirt. She'd kissed me. I'd pulled away. I'd tried to move her off me. But then she threatened me again, threatened Avory and Cash. Somehow, she knew *everything*. She knew Avory and I had been together since she was fifteen. She knew Cash had been lying, had been pretending to be me. She had names of all the girls we'd made the switch on. She'd done her research, the fucking stalker.

She wanted one kiss in exchange for her silence. So I'd kissed her.

And that one kiss had wrecked my whole fucking world.

"Hey."

"Avory?" I stood, nearly flying out of the old overstuffed chair, knocking over the empty beer bottles at my feet. We'd always come out here together near the gate at the back of the compound. So that was where I'd been for the last five nights, hoping I'd see her. She was standing a few yards away now, her perfect hands clasped in front of her tiny shorts almost covered by an oversize t-shirt. Her feet were bare, like she'd climbed out of bed and her window desperate to get to me. "Holy shit, baby, I—"

She held her hand up, cutting me off. "I'm going to talk first."

I nodded, not really in any position to argue with her. I missed the sound of her voice. I missed the sight of her. I missed the feel of her flesh against mine. I missed every single fucking thing about loving Avory Connor.

"It's over, Crue. It's so fucking over. I trusted you. I loved you. I *worshipped* you. And you cheated on me." She licked her lips, tears pooling in her gorgeous eyes. "We could have come clean to our parents, we could have asked our family for help. We could have fucking packed our bags and run away. But instead, you shut me out, you went on a date, and you hooked up with the whore who was blackmailing you."

I stepped forward, prepared to fall to my knees in front of her. "Baby, I didn't hook up with her. It was one kiss. I swear. I know it looks so much worse in the photos, but she had pictures of us and she was going to—"

"I don't care," she screamed into the darkness, her face going red as her tears started to fall freely. "I don't care if it was one kiss. And I don't care if she had fucking HD video of us fucking in an empty field. I don't care. I don't trust you. It's over."

"Avory, baby, please."

"Stop." She held her hand up, her voice going soft. "You broke my heart, and you broke us." She took a deep breath, squaring her shoulders. "I'm not my sister. I won't cry any more tears over you. I won't spend the rest of my life mourning what we had. I'll smile at family dinners. I'll act like nothing is wrong. I'll be the happy outgoing girl I've always been, and our parents will have no fucking clue that you ripped my soul from my fucking chest."

We were both crying now, both panting, heaving with loss. I never knew I could hurt this bad. I never knew I could feel so fucking low. She didn't care that I did what I did to save us, to save Cash. She didn't care that I'd done my best to fix what I'd broken between my twin and me.

"I don't trust you anymore, Crue, and without that trust, we have nothing."

Chapter Three

Avory

Now

I was half naked, standing in front of the bathroom mirror finishing my makeup, getting ready for Friday Family Dinner, which Colin insisted we go to. I didn't mind skipping every now and then, but ever since I'd let my current boyfriend meet my large chaotic family, we'd been to every one of the noisy get-togethers. Colin was an only child, and he was captivated with the Devil's Share and their many spawn. We were three generations now, and growing by the year.

I loved my family, and I enjoyed being around them, but once a week as an overflowing unit was sometimes a little much.

"Sweetie, are you ready to go? We need to leave now if we don't want to be late to dinner."

I turned as he stepped into the bathroom, a flirty smirk on my face. "Or we could be late on purpose." I crooked my finger, teasing him. I was wearing tight jeans and a lacy white bra that, I had to admit, looked damn appealing.

"That would be rude." He leaned forward, kissing my forehead gently. "I need your family to love me, sweetie. I need them to be okay with me whisking you across the country."

I nodded, waiting until he left before I let my smile fall. Colin was nice, kind, generous, and brilliant. He treated me like a princess. He had values, tons of them. And he'd been offered a once-in-a-lifetime job, in Portland, Oregon. He'd asked me to go with him seven days ago and I still hadn't given him my final answer. I told him I needed time to think about it, time to talk to my family. But in his mind, he and I were a done deal, and there was no way I would turn him down.

Part of me wanted to be all in, wanted to go with him and start over. It'd be a clean slate, a fresh start. I'd earned it, and it would probably do me a world of good. But another part of me wanted to stay. I wanted to be with my family. I wanted to watch all the little babies grow up. I *wanted* to be annoyed by constant family dinners.

I finished getting dressed, pulling an old cut-up Clashing Swell concert shirt on with my jeans. I let Colin take my hand and lead me out to the hybrid he drove, getting in after he opened the door for me. He was polite and chivalrous. He was handsome in a way that had never appealed to me before. He needed glasses to see one foot in front of him and his hair was constantly a mess. He wore ironic t-shirts that I didn't always understand and old Chucks that looked like they'd been run over by an eighteen-wheeler. But somehow it all worked for me. He was refreshing. He was exactly what I needed in my life. Exactly the type of guy I should want. But for some reason, I was less than thrilled with his proposition.

"Hey, please don't bring up the move tonight." I placed my hand on top of his where it rested on my knee. "I need to talk to Jett and Marley about working remotely, and I need to talk to my parents." *And I'm not entirely sure I want to move across the country with you.* "Okay?"

He brought our joined hand to his lips, kissing mine sweetly. "Of course. I understand."

He was also incredibly understanding. Had I mentioned that yet? I was a bit of a brat, always had been. But Colin never called me on it. He navigated my moods like someone bobbing and weaving an onslaught of red rubber dodge balls.

Moving was my choice, and I knew that if I chose to stay in Texas he wouldn't hate me. He'd be understanding and kind, and probably suggest we try long distance. He loved me, and for that, I was a lucky girl.

"Thank you."

"I know you'll miss all those sweet babies, all those baby spawn." He paused to chuckle at his own joke. "But I promise, we'll visit all the time."

Baby spawn. That'd been me once upon a time. I squeezed Colin's hand, turning to look out the window while memories came creeping into the edges of my mind. It'd been so long since I let myself think about Crue Matthews as anything other than an infuriatingly permanent fixture in my family. Why today? I was guessing any psych major would tell you it was because I had a great guy sitting next to me, being kind and understanding, and asking me for the rest of my life, and I was hesitating.

"Sneaking out is an interesting hobby, baby spawn."

I stopped short, trying real hard not to let Crue Matthews know that he had startled me. "Yeah? So is stalking." *I was sneaking off the compound, and this was the second time he'd been down here during my night flight indiscretions. The first time, he'd caught me coming home well past curfew.*

He was sitting in the old chair Landry had used to climb over the fence when she was sneaking out after she was supposed to be tucked safely in bed. The rest of us kids had gone for broke and simply cut a giant hole in the fencing. "Don't flatter yourself, I wasn't waiting for you."

I wanted him *to be waiting for me. I wanted* him *to care. I wanted* him *to be jealous, and none of it made any fucking sense. I'd had guys drooling over me since freshman year, and yet the only one I was interested in was off limits and uninterested.*

"Smoking and stalking. Even better," *I shot back with my typical sassiness, not wanting him to know he mattered.*

"You meeting someone?" Crue held up the joint between his fingers, closer to my face.

His offer felt intimate. I schooled my face, not wanting him to know my heart was racing. I leaned forward, taking the smoke deep into my lungs and holding my breath as I responded with a strangled, "Yes."

"Cancel."

I blew out a long breath, the smoke thinned and curling in front of my face. "What?" *Had I heard him right? The words had been spoken harshly, more like a demand than a request, and his tone made my blood start to heat in my veins. I coughed lightly, clearing the haze from my chest.* "Why?"

Why. *That was the million-dollar question, wasn't it? Why did he want me to cancel my plans? Why did I want to do exactly as he commanded?*

"You really think this one is going to be any different than the last one?" The last one? The guy he'd caught bringing me home the other night. Why was Crue watching me? Was he jealous? "Think

he's going to give you what you're looking for?" He spoke softly, barely a whisper into the dark night. But what he said carried weight, like an arrow straight to my rebellious, confused little heart.

"Maybe. What does it matter? You the only one of us allowed to sneak out and hook up?" It hurt every time I saw him with another girl, and had for the last year or so. I wasn't sure when my crush on a boy I was raised to see as family began, but it was like a snowball rolling downhill, gaining momentum until it had knocked me flat on my ass and left me out of breath.

He held the joint up again, letting me dip down and take another hit. "You really wanna be like me, baby spawn?"

Silence settled between us as I held the smoke deep in my lungs. I wasn't the baby of the family, and I didn't want him to see me that way. I exhaled a few moments later, kicking his feet off the old stump they were resting on so I could sit down. "I don't know who I want to be yet."

Did any of us? Life here on the Devil's Share compound didn't give you much time to think about the direction you wanted to take or who you wanted to be when you grew up. It was loud and chaotic, and since I was constantly surrounded by other people it was hard to know where they stopped and I began.

Crue reached around me, plucking my cell out of my back pocket. "Cancel your plans, Avory."

My eyes met his, my tongue darting out to wet my lips. There was that tone again, that commanding edge to his voice that made me want to listen. That made me want to do each and every little thing he told me to. I nodded, breaking our connection to type out a quick message to the already forgotten guy who was supposed to come pick me up. "Done." I rose to my feet, feeling antsy and nervous. We were alone in the dark, only the smoky haze between us. I had a crush on him and for the first time, I was starting to suspect he had one on me too. "Now what, Crue?"

He stared up at me, studying my face, like he was searching for answers. I didn't back away. I didn't look down. When he grabbed my hips and jerked me into his lap, I was so fucking game. His lips crashed against mine, instantly destroying our relationship and rebuilding it into something new at the same time. My hands fisted his shirt, pulling him closer as soft moans escaped my mouth. He wanted me the same way I wanted him. And neither of us seemed to care that it didn't make any fucking sense.

Chapter Four

Crue

Now

I crossed the compound, headed to the pool house for Friday Family Dinner. I didn't make it every week. I skipped out on a lot of these. I was a sullen asshole, and had been for years now. Although I'd always been a bit of a prick, ask anyone in my family. The sulky heartbroken version of me had been firmly in place since my breakup with Avory Connor. I'd sunk into a deep depression, and I'd never seemed to be able to shake it all the way off.

Don't get me wrong. I had a good life. I went out. I drank with my buddies and hooked up with random chicks every now and then. I played catch with my twin and cheered him on during every major league game I could get to. I smoked with my younger brother, laughing about our childhood. I played with my little cousins. I made them giggle and held them high in the air whenever they begged me to. I hung out with my dad in the backyard, standing over the grill. I brought my mom flowers on her birthday and Mother's Day.

I lived.

But my heart hurt. I still mourned the girl I lost. And every time I saw her across the table, I hated myself for what I did to her. To us.

"Hey, man, I didn't know you were coming to dinner tonight." Jett held the wrought iron gate open for me, letting it slam shut as soon as I passed through.

"Our brother is telling the family he's going to be a dad, why would you think I'd miss that?" Like I said, I tended to skip more Devil's Share functions than any of my other cousins or siblings, but this? I wouldn't miss this. Only Jett and I knew that Katie was pregnant, and she and Cash had this big reveal thing they were going to do at family dinner. Cash thought it'd be funny, actually sharing happy news over a meal instead of the truth bombs and drama that usually ensued.

"I thought you'd miss it because Avory is here."

Enter the actual pain in my chest. Avory was the only girl I'd ever loved, and the only girl who had ever broken my heart. I'd broken hers first. I shrugged, hoping for unaffected. "What does that matter? I see Avory all the time."

And it hurt, all the damn time.

"She's bringing that same guy she's been seeing."

My eyebrows rose, shocked that Avory had stuck with the same dude for so long. Typically she brought them around once or twice, then we never had to see them again. "The same one who was here for the holidays? The weird hipster who tried to pick a fight with me?"

"You mean the tech genius environmentalist who peacefully avoided your rampant anger? Yeah, that one." Jett nodded, his hands shoved in his pockets.

So the guy was brilliant and going out of his way to save the damn planet. That didn't mean he wasn't a weird hipster. And he'd totally thrown digs my way. "Whatever, bro. Avory's been flaunting her flings all over the damn compound from the second we broke up. This one's no different."

Jett sent me a small smile with a look in his eyes that resembled pity as he walked away. I didn't need his pity. I didn't need anyone's. I chose to be here for Cash and Katie like they'd been there for me. I could handle Avory bringing a date. I could handle her laughing loudly at his lame jokes and running her fingers down his arm. I could handle it all. Because I knew that whomever she brought around was nothing but a cheap substitute. No one would be able to replace me in her heart, and in her soul, the same way no one would be able to replace her in mine.

Avory and I were once in a lifetime. No one would ever be able to love her like I did. And deep down, she knew it too.

I watched as Jett made his way to Marley, taking her son into his arms and smacking kisses on his chubby cheeks. The baby giggled, grabbing handfuls of Jett's dark hair. Talon stepped closer to his wife, wrapping his arms tightly around her.

The whole family was here and it was crowded. I could hear my dad in the corner talking with Uncle Jacks about an expansion project since everyone kept popping out kids and getting married, most of them in that order because we sneered at tradition. We were outgrowing the space the 'rents had built for us to gather as a whole.

It was the Connors' week to bring the food, which meant dinner was being catered because Aunt Lexi was the worst cook on the compound. They'd chosen to have a crawfish boil and there were white butcher-paper tablecloths covering the extra-long picnic tables. The large stainless steel pots full of potatoes, corn, and crawfish were stationed outside the main deck so none of the toddlers got hurt.

Cash and Katie were joined at the hip, which wasn't anything out of the ordinary. Cash was playing pro ball and for over half the year, he was gone more than he was home. Honestly, I wasn't sure when Cash had found the time to knock her up with his schedule the way it'd been. It was hard on them, but at least here at the compound Katie was never truly alone. Her little brother even lived in town now with our cousin Emmie and their baby girl Luca.

I made sure to check on her too, having dinner with her once a week, calling and texting all the time. I'd promised Cash I'd be here for her, help with the pregnancy when he was out of town. And I would. Katie was like a sister to me, had been good to me, and I would do anything for her and my twin.

Landry and Halen were by the pool gate thwarting their kids' attempts to go for a swim. Between the two of them, they had four. Three boys and a girl, and Halen was pregnant again. Constant freaking babies popping out in this family.

Emmie and Evie were with their mom, cooing over Luca. Nicky and Kasen were standing off to the side with Uncle Smith, their father-in-law. I'd held a bit of a grudge for my uncle after he'd decided to share the picture of me with that chick in high school. I'd tried to get to Avory first. I'd tried to pull her away. I thought if I could explain things, if I could make her understand… But that was not how it went down, and I'd never know if it would've made a difference in the end. The resentment at Uncle Smith stuck though. Better to be pissed at him than myself, though, truth? I beat myself up plenty.

Avory was talking to Dylan, laughing at whatever Jett's girlfriend had said. She was close with them, and had started working for MJ Botanicals after she graduated from UT with a degree in graphic design.

Colin. That was the hipster's name. I refused to call him her boyfriend. I refused to even think for a second that he was going to be a permanent member of this family. He was fleeting. Everyone in her life was fleeting, except me. He was standing next to her, holding her glass of wine and his beer. He seemed like one of those guys who would take off his jacket and lay it down over the top of a puddle so Avory wouldn't get her shoes dirty. I chuckled at the image in my head. Me? I would've picked her ass up and thrown her over my shoulder, carrying her over the puddle and straight to the back seat of my truck.

Aunt Lexi cupped her hands around her mouth, and called out, "Dinner is served." The catering crew poured steaming piles of food on the table, a long line of deep red crawfish and bright yellow corn. It looked amazing, and smelled even better.

I hung back, letting the rest of my family find their spot at the table. Cash caught my eye, gesturing me over with his head. He stepped closer to Katie, making room for me between her and Brody. I loved Jett, obviously, but Brody was probably my second favorite "brother." He was a hella likeable guy, and he was always fucking grinning.

Uncle Smith started dinner the way he'd been doing since Kase had proposed to a pregnant Emmie. "Unless anyone has anything they've been hiding from us to get off their chest, dinner is—"

"We have something we've been hiding." Cash's smile was megawatt as he held his and Katie's joined hands in the air. "We're pregnant."

I knew about the baby. I'd actually been at their house when Katie found out. She'd screamed and came running out of the bathroom waving the test stick in the air. Now, I stepped back, letting everyone else have a chance to congratulate them. My eyes drifted to Avory, who was beaming, waiting in line to hug my twin and his wife. Her hair was still long, her frame still slender. But she'd gotten more beautiful as she grew up all the way. Her grin fell and she looked across the patio, meeting my gaze. I wondered if she was thinking the same thing I was: that it could have been us happily married, announcing a baby through joyful tears.

"You want kids?" Avory ran her hands through my hair, tugging playfully when I wrinkled my nose in disgust. "Are you serious?"

I was lying in her lap, on a blanket under the stars at the back of the compound. It'd become our place, and I was more than happy to share it with her. "I don't know. I've spent the majority of my formative years trying real fucking hard to not procreate."

"Hmmm, I love when you bring up what a fuck boy you used to be." She slapped my cheek, harder than one would have thought necessary. "Warms me to my core."

I launched myself up, tackling her to the ground and grinning when she wrapped her long legs around my hips. "I bet I could figure out a different way to warm you to your core." I kissed her lips, hungry for every taste I could get. Sneaking around meant lying to our parents, but it also meant that we were alone a lot and that was a win.

"Answer me first. Honestly, do you want kids?" Avory was peering up at me, her gaze searching mine.

She was so fucking beautiful, and I was in love with her. Fuck, I loved that girl. I kissed her again, grinding against her core because I could. But then I pulled back, smiling down at the only girl who had ever owned me. "Do you want babies?" She nodded, a soft, sweet look in her big brown eyes. "Then I'll give them to you."

I blinked, turning my back on the happy family scene in front of me. Not only could it have been us, but once upon a time I was sure it would be. And as ecstatic as I was for my twin and for Katie, part of my heart was breaking for everything I still longed for.

Chapter Five

Crue

Now

While most everyone had gone to bed, Brody, Jett, Talon, Cash, and I were sitting on Cash's back patio around the fire pit. We were passing around a congratulatory bottle of whiskey and shooting the shit. I'd taken time like this with my brothers for granted when I was younger. Hell, I'd taken most things for granted. Cash traveled a lot, Talon and Jett were busy with MJ Botanicals, and Brody was at home with his sons, Mr. Mom all the way. There wasn't a lot of time for late-night fireside chats so I was trying like hell to soak up this one.

"Avory can't be serious with that guy, right? I mean he looks like a strong wind could blow him over." Cash was forever on my side, because he was loyal to a fault. He knew I still loved Avory, and he knew that even though I played it cool, seeing her with someone else bruised my perpetually hurt heart.

"She's really serious." Jett had a live crawfish in his hand. He'd decided he wanted to keep one as a pet. And Devin, the sweetest girl alive, had found an old fishbowl so he could fill it with dirt and water. "They stopped by the house after dinner and—"

"Don't even think about him, bro." Brody clapped me on the back. "He's not worth the head space, okay?" Brody was the "outsider" I was closest to, other than Katie. He and I had clicked almost instantly, even though we were so opposite. I guess he evened me out like Cash tended to do.

"But he is, that's what I'm trying to tell you guys." Jett dropped his new pet into its home, and then plucked a pill bug off the deck and dropped it in there with it. "What do crawfish eat? You know what, never mind, I'll look it up later." He sat the bowl down and then turned to look at the rest of us. "Like I was saying, Avory came by with Colin."

"Don't use his name." I was being childish, and I'd had enough whiskey not to care. "Don't call him her boyfriend either."

"Fine." Jett sighed at my immature demand. "Avory's *special friend* got this amazing job offer in Portland, and he asked Avory to go with him."

I scoffed. "Avory would never leave Texas. She loves all you assholes way too much. She has nieces and nephews, her new job with MJ Botanicals. She's not going to move across the country to be with that douche." I wasn't concerned, not in the slightest. I knew Avory. I knew what she valued, what mattered to her. She wouldn't leave her family. She wouldn't leave us.

"Crue." Jett's gaze darted to Cash, then back to me. "That's why they stopped by to talk to me. Avory wanted to know if she would be able to work for MJ Botanicals remotely."

Remotely? She was going with him? I stopped breathing. My heart stopped beating, everything I needed to survive ceased functioning. The patio fell silent for a few moments while everyone absorbed Jett's words the way I was struggling to do.

"You're with family, and Talon, bro, let it out." Jett got to his feet, leaving his crawfish fishbowl on the deck. "Scream, cry, lose your shit."

I barely registered it as Talon rolled his eyes at Jett's joke, excluding him as family. "I don't even know how you've held it together this long. I thought when she brought him to Christmas your head was going to explode."

Yeah, Christmas had sucked. But this? This was a punch to the fucking balls.

"No." I shook my head, trying to drag air into my lungs. "No. She's not moving with him. She's not leaving. She can't. She won't. She doesn't love him. I know she doesn't love him."

How could she? How could she love him when she was still in love with me? A love like ours didn't disappear like that. It didn't fade away. It couldn't be replaced. I'd never be able to replace her, so she shouldn't be able to replace me. Right?

Jett nodded sagely. "Ah, *denial*, that's how you've kept your cool."

"It's not denial," I snapped, getting to my feet, the need to escape my audience clawing at my throat with angry nails. "She doesn't love him." They didn't understand. They didn't know how Avory and I felt about each other. "She's still angry at me, but she'll come around."

"Still angry? Crue, it's been like five years, man." The look Brody trained on me was one of veiled wariness. "I don't want you to Hulk out on me or anything, but maybe it's…over."

Things between Avory and I weren't over. There was still love there lingering between us. I could feel it every time she accidentally brushed against my body, every time her eyes stayed on mine a few seconds longer than necessary. Our love was epic, and epic love didn't get snuffed out with one tragic fight.

"No." I bounded down the back steps, leaving the faint light of the porch and heading into the darkness of the compound. I couldn't stay there. I couldn't stand their pity, their ignorance.

It wasn't over. It would never be over. Avory was made for me, and I was made for her. We were that forever kind of love.

"Do you ever feel bad sneaking into my bedroom after my parents have gone to sleep?"

Was that a fucking trick question? I couldn't help but chuckle softly as I answered her. "Nope." I shut her window, almost all the way. "If your parents didn't want deviants coming into their house after lights out, they should be more aware of their surroundings."

She smiled and my chest swelled. I'd fallen in love with everything about Avory Connor. I loved her sass, her defiance. I loved the way she let me touch her. I loved her trust. I loved that this thing between us made no fucking sense but neither one of us seemed to care. I'd been sneaking into her room for a few nights now, no longer satisfied with a couple stolen hours making out down by the back gate. I wanted more. I wanted more time, more touches. I wanted to own her, the way she owned me.

She sat up, her sheets pooling in her lap, her short sleep shirt barely covering her torso. Avory didn't like to wear a lot of clothes. I loved that about her too. She was wholly herself. She didn't give a damn what anyone else thought. "You gonna do more than kiss me tonight, Crue Matthews?"

"I've already done more than kiss you. You need a reminder?" I dropped to my knees, fully prepared to feast on my girl.

"I want more," she whispered into the night, making chills race down my spine. "I want it all."

I did too. But for the first time in my life, I was afraid that wanting it all would ruin everything. "We have all the time in the world, baby spawn. Don't rush on my account." I'd been with more girls than I ever wanted to say out loud in front of Avory, even though I was sure she already knew. But with her, I didn't feel the urgency to get to the finish line.

"Do I ever do anything for anyone's account beside my own?" She rose up on her knees, the moonlight bright enough for me to catch her lacy black panties.

Avory knew what she wanted and she tended to go after it, no matter the consequences. She and I were a lot alike: we were so different from the rest of our family. They were selfless, self-deprecating, and they always put others above themselves. The only person I'd ever put before me was Avory. And maybe my twin, every now and then.

She reached for me, gripping my athletic shorts and using the waistband to drag me toward her. I sighed, shaking my head playfully. "Such the little brat." I picked her up, tossing her back against her pillows. Her eyes stayed on mine, watching as I let my shorts fall to my bare feet.

"I'm a brat, and you're an asshole."

She wasn't wrong. We both owned who we were and didn't feel the need to apologize. We were made for each other, like two pieces of the same semi-fucked-up whole. I grabbed her hips, dragging her down the bed and underneath me. "You wouldn't want me any other way."

Avory had shocked me the first time we'd made out. She'd bit my lip and pretty much came apart when I'd pulled her hair in response. She wasn't delicate, and she made sure I knew it. Which worked real fucking well for me, because I didn't do soft and sweet.

"You're right. Now be an asshole and give me what I want."

I tore her panties down one side, then the other. "You always get your way."

She scraped her nails down my bare chest, leaving pink lines in her wake. "You going to lie to me and tell me you don't want this?"

I shook my head. "I'll never lie to you, baby." I ground myself against her core, loving the hiss that escaped her lips. I held still *after that, waiting until her eyes flew open in annoyance. "I love you, you know that, right?" She nodded, her expression going soft. "In order for me to love you the way you want to be loved, I need you to trust me."*

"I do trust you." She reached up, cupping my cheek, and I placed a kiss on her palm. "I promise, Crue, I trust you. I love you."

We were sarcastic jerks, even to each other half the time, but in this moment I needed more. I needed her to know that I cherished her, that this wasn't some fling for me. She meant something. Something big, and I wanted her trust as much as I wanted her love. I never wanted her to regret us.

I positioned the head of my cock at her entrance, my eyes connected to hers. "Say it again, Avory."

"I trust you." She knew that was what I wanted to hear.

I pulled back and slammed inside of her tight pussy, crashing through her barrier without remorse. Loving my girl exactly the way she wanted to be loved.

Chapter Six

Avory

Now

I was still at my parents' house. My dad had offered, and Colin had insisted we stay the weekend. He was such a people pleaser. Which wasn't a bad trait, it was a good thing. Putting other people's needs and feelings in front of your own. He was selfless: his behavior commendable. But at the same time, it made me wonder. Could I spend the rest of my life with someone like him?

Ugh. I needed to stop. I loved Colin, I did. And before he'd asked me to move away with him, I'd been incredibly happy in our relationship. But it was like he'd suddenly put us in warp speed and it'd freaked me the hell out.

I adored my family and the thought of leaving them literally made my heart ache. I'd known one home my whole life. The condo I owned in Austin was the first place I'd lived off the compound. I was used to being surrounded by my sisters and cousins, their babies climbing all over me at every meal. I even worked for a family business.

"Hey, there you are." Colin stepped onto my parents' back porch, sitting down next to me in one of the outside lounge chairs. He'd been inside helping my dad fix his computer and I'd been sitting in the warm sunshine trying to thaw my freezing heart. "We haven't gotten a chance to talk since last night when Jett said you could work remotely."

"I'll need a home office and a secure VPN."

"Lucky for you, your boyfriend is a tech mastermind." He took my hand in his, bringing it to his lips for a quick kiss. "What was next on that list of yours? You needed to talk to your parents?"

He was so hopeful, so eager. He wanted me with him. He wanted to start a life together. I should be jumping for joy, packing my bags while whistling a merry little tune. But I still wasn't sure. I didn't know if I wanted to move. I didn't know if I wanted to spend the rest of my life with Colin. Because that was what this step would mean to him. It would mean forever. I knew that.

"Uh, yeah, there are a few conversations I need to have." But right now, I wanted to escape *this* conversation. I wanted to escape the hopeful lilt in his voice. I needed some space to think, to figure out what I wanted. "In fact, I'm going to go have one of them now." I got to my feet, smiling down at the man who I should say yes to. "You going to be okay here for a bit?"

He nodded, kissing the back of my hand once again. "Of course, sweetie, do what you need to do."

***

My younger sister was the most brutally honest person I'd ever met in my entire life. When I needed real advice, when I needed to be called on my bullshit, she was where I went. She'd helped me start dating again after Crue and I broke up. She'd helped me pick a major, and she'd talked me out of running for office in my sorority. I tended to fly into situations without thinking them through all the way, but Marley was born skeptical and jaded, and I needed her to guide me through life's mazes.

I knocked twice, then walked into her newly built home across the road from the Devil's Share compound. Talon's car was over at MJ Botanicals, so I figured Marley was here somewhere with their son. Co was a carbon copy of his dad, thank goodness. He was happy, sweet, always smiling, and kind.

"Yo, MVP, where you at?" I passed through the entryway, checking the kitchen and the living room.

"Back here. Your nephew just shit in the bathtub. Come help me." I laughed as I rounded the corner, heading toward the master bedroom and Marley's voice. She was holding her son up out of the tub, water dripping off his little naked body. "Take him, I'll start disinfecting."

I took him, wrapping him in a fluffy green towel with an alligator hood before sitting on the ground and settling him in my lap. Co was a super content kid, happy to be held by his aunt. He'd sit in my lap for an hour straight if I wanted him to. In short, he was absolutely nothing like Brody and Landry's tornado children.

"I need your advice."

"You want my advice? When you have kids, hire a nanny." Marley poured half a gallon of bleach into the tub, soaking all the bath toys that had been affected by the dump her kid had taken in the middle of bath time. She rocked back on her heels, blowing a loose dark strand of hair out of her face. "I'm sorry, it's been a morning. What's up?"

"I can't decide if I should go with Colin or stay in Texas." I rested my chin lightly on top of Co's green 'gator-covered head. I'd gone to talk to Jett last night about working remotely because staff was his domain, but I knew that he would have told Marley what was going on by now.

Marley sat on the tile next to me, handing Co a toy from the floor that hadn't been part of the bath mess. "You answered your own question, Avory."

I turned to look at her, my eyebrows raised in confusion. "Spell it out for your big sister, MVP."

"You can't decide if you *should* go or stay. *Should* implies that you think of moving to Portland with Colin as an obligation or a chore. Something you're *supposed* to do, not necessarily something you *want* to do." I rested my head on her shoulder, knowing that she was as right as rain, per usual. "Avory, if you aren't excited at the idea of going with Colin, then it's not the right choice. And you know it. You wanted to hear it from someone else so you didn't feel so shitty about it."

I did feel shitty. She was right again. "I don't know *why* I don't want to go. Colin is great. He's brilliant and kind, he treats me like royalty and—"

"And he bores the ever-loving hell out of you." She got to her feet and lifted Co onto her hip. "Come on, I need to get a diaper on him before he shits on the floor next."

I followed her into her bedroom, tickling my nephew's tummy as soon as she placed him on her bed. "Colin is the nicest guy I've ever dated."

"He's the smartest too." Marley quickly slipped a diaper on her son, then put him on the floor so he could play with the pile of wooden blocks on the ground. "Colin will be okay, Avory. He'll move to Portland, make great money, and do wonderful things for the world. It won't take long for him to meet a girl who worships him and makes him forget all about the rock-and-roll princess who broke his heart."

The thought of him forgetting about me didn't bother me. Which said it all, didn't it? I wanted him to forget me, to move on. I wanted him to be smitten with someone else so I didn't have to feel any guilt. I didn't deserve his kindness. "I was happy with him, before he asked me to move. I swear I was." I got excited every time I saw him. I missed him when we were apart. I was falling for him, slowly, but still I was falling. "But then he asked me to move and everything started to change."

"Of course it did." Marley rolled her eyes like I was the densest person on the damn planet. "You were happy with him because there was no pressure. You were exploring what it was like to be with a good guy. You were caught up in the newness. But the moment it became real, the moment he was asking for more, you fucking balked."

Accurate. I'd felt immediately on edge and trapped from the moment he'd told me about his promotion. But then again, maybe I'd *balked* because he was asking me to leave my comfort zone? And never straying from what I was used to didn't send all that healthy either. "Moving might be good for me. Maybe..."

"Look. You came to me because you knew I'd be honest with you. I don't mince words. I don't even know how." She picked Co up off the floor, hiking him back onto her hip. "Colin loves you more than you love him. When Cash and Katie announced that they were having a baby, you didn't turn to your boyfriend with hearts in your eyes. You gave him your back and looked at Crue."

I opened my mouth to protest, to tell her she was wrong, but she held her hand up. "Whether you meant to or not, you did. Colin doesn't hold your attention anymore, and he doesn't deserve your pity love. So stop thinking about what would be good for *you*, and for at least one time in your relationship, think about what would be best for him."

I wracked my brain, looking for a rebuttal. Searching for a time when I put Colin first, when I was a good girlfriend. But I had nothing. I sighed, pursing my lips. "And here I thought I'd worked on myself as a person."

She made me sound like a selfish monster, which sucked a whole lot. But maybe she was right. Not about me looking at Crue at dinner, that didn't happen the way she thought it did. I was watching Cash, watching how excited he was. And *he* looked over at Crue. I simply followed his gaze. I wasn't staring at my first love thinking about how it could have been us. I was watching one of my best friends worry about his twin in a moment when he should have only been thinking of himself and his growing family.

"You're my sister and I love you. Co adores you, all the kids do. You show up, you love your family. You're a hard worker, and color me shocked, but you've become an invaluable asset to MJ Botanicals."

Marley left her bedroom, knowing I would follow so I could hear her say more nice things about me. Although I was positive there was a but coming. "You are a good person, Avory, you are. But sometimes," there it was, "you get so wrapped up in your own shit that you forget there are other people being affected by your actions."

I scoffed, taking my nephew from her so she could make his naptime bottle with two hands. "Is this still about the summer I convinced you to let me dye your hair blonde?" I was joking, trying to lighten the mood. And she knew it.

"I'll never forgive you." She lost the battle with the scowl she was sporting and broke into a smile. "Brat." She went back to making her baby's bottle, her voice growing softer. "You know, if you stay, Crue is going to think it's because of him."

"It won't be." If I stayed in Texas, if I ended things with Colin, it would be for me. Well, for me and for Colin because he deserved more than what I could give him. Crue didn't factor into my decisions, my life choices. He hadn't for a really long time. "Thanks for the talk. I knew I could count on you to help me figure out my shit."

"You knew the right answer already, Avory. You just needed confirmation because somewhere along the way, you lost trust in yourself." She took Co from my arms and handed him his warm milk. "One day you'll grow up and stop seeking validation from other people." She wasn't being rude or unkind: she was being

Marley. She spoke with no filter, but she also spoke with no judgment, so it evened out. "I love you."

"Love you too, MVP." I stepped forward, cupping my nephew's chubby cheek and smacking a kiss on his forehead. "And I love you, sweet boy."

Chapter Seven

Avory

Now

Marley was right. I'd known what I needed to do from the moment Colin had asked me to move with him. I'd never been excited about the idea. No part of me had ever really wanted to go. My life was here in Texas. Not with Colin. And he didn't need to carry me across the country with him like a weight around his neck.

When I got back to the compound, he was on the couch watching football with my dad. There were bowls of chips on the coffee table and iced tea sweating on coasters. It was cliché, but totally what a Sunday in any of our homes looked like. But Colin hated football, sports of any kind really. Which should've told me something about compatibility. He was all brain, all heart. And I didn't deserve him.

"Hey, sweetie, you're back." Colin held his hand out, wanting me to come to him. "You want to watch the game with your dad and me?" His eyes got large, like he was trying to silently ask me to get him out of it.

"Yeah, come on, baby girl, watch the game with your old man and your new man." When my dad said shit like that, I had a hard time imagining him as a fuck boy rock star before he met my mom. Mentally sighing, I watched my dad pat the couch between them, a loving grin on his face. They were both so happy to see me, but one of them was about to lose their smile.

"Actually, uh, can I talk to you for a minute? Alone." I gestured with my head to the back patio and Colin's grateful smile made me feel like the biggest jerk on the planet. He thought he was getting a better deal, no more football and a few moments alone with his girlfriend. Instead, he was about to be dumped.

My dad's eyes tracked us as we stepped out back, leaning forward in his seat until he almost fell out of it. I shut the door, blocking his view. He was my father. He knew my tone didn't say good things. I was rarely soft and sweet. I was more sassy and snarky.

"Thank you for getting me out of there. I know nothing about football and your dad kept asking me all these questions I couldn't answer." Colin took my hand, bringing it to his lips for a kiss. "You want to go for a walk? It's such a beautiful day."

He turned, looking out over my family's land. My parents' backyard faced a field full of tall switch grass, and when the wind blew, the grass's swaying rhythms became almost hypnotic. The tank was over a small ridge, and then the red barn beyond that. "Maybe we could build a little place here too, that way when we came to visit, we'd have our own space." He pointed while shielding his eyes from the glare of the setting sun. "Isn't that barn empty now that Marley and Jett live across the street? Do you think your parents would be okay if we renovated it?"

That barn wasn't empty. And the person who lived there would rather burn it down than let Colin and I make it our home.

"Colin." He had to stop talking about our future. It was killing me and making me... Nope. I was being a selfish brat again. This wasn't about me. This was about him. "I can't go with you to Portland."

He spun to face me, a frown on his handsome face. "What?"

"I, uh, I thought about it a lot and it's not right." I was fidgeting, my hands twisting in front of me. I rarely fidgeted, but this conversation was harder than I thought it would be. "My family is here, my job is here. I just started with MJ Botanicals, my sisters are popping out babies left and right, and—"

"I'll turn down the job." Colin shook his head, his voice cracking. "I'll stay here with you. I don't want the job if you aren't there with me. Money isn't important, people are important. You want to stay with your family, then I'll stay too."

Oh holy shit. I closed my eyes, cursing my cold dead heart. Why, world? Why couldn't I be head over heels in love with this man? He's amazing. He's everything. But he's not for me, and I needed to get this conversation the hell over with.

"Colin, no. Go to Portland, take the once-in-a-lifetime job." I took a deep breath, stepping closer to the heart I was about to break. "You're a great guy. You're an actual dream come true. But you deserve better than me. More. You deserve someone who wouldn't hesitate to say yes, someone who is all in. Someone who would put you first. And that's not me. I'm sorry."

He blinked rapidly, his green eyes almost crossing in confusion. "Wait. So you're not moving to Portland *and* you're breaking up with me?" His hands went to his hips. "No long distance, no let's see how it goes? Just, I'm not coming, you shouldn't stay, and I'm not the girl for you?"

I nodded. That was the gist of it right there.

"I thought, uh, I thought we were in this together. I thought we were in love." He looked back across the field, taking a shaky breath. "Was it something I did? Is there someone else?"

"Yes." His eyes shot up to meet mine. "I mean there is someone else." I shrugged, being as honest as I'd ever been. "Me." I should have recorded this shit for Marley to see me evolving as a person. "I'm selfish. I'm a brat. We both know it."

"Sweetie, you're not a brat, you're, uh, a bit, uh, difficult at times." He reached for my hands, a pleading tone taking over the barely contained despair from earlier. "It doesn't bother me, you know that. I love taking care of you. I love you."

"Dude." I sighed. "You should be with someone who takes care of *you*. You shouldn't have to navigate my moods. I'm the worst. Really, I am. Ask anyone in my family." I threw my hands wide, then dropped them, letting them slap against my thighs. "I'm standing here, trying to put your needs before mine and you're still outshining me. Go to Oregon, Colin, find a great girl, fall in love."

"I am in love."

Jesus H. Christ. I'd never dumped anyone I cared about before, except Crue. This was proving to be quite difficult. "Colin, it's over. I'll leave the house so you can pack up your things. You have a key to my apartment. I'll stay here on the compound until you can get your stuff from there too. Take all the time you need."

He stared at me for a solid sixty seconds before brushing past me and going back inside. I felt sick to my stomach, but I also felt lighter. I'd done the right thing for both of us.

One day, he'd look up at the clouds and thank whoever was listening that Avory Connor had dumped him on her parents' back porch.

***

I spent the rest of the afternoon avoiding the 'rents. I knew they'd have questions, and they'd baby me and ask if I was all right. I didn't deserve their kindness. I broke a good guy's heart and I deserved to feel like an asshole for a while.

Asshole.

"I'm a brat, and you're an asshole."

"And you wouldn't want it any other way."

Marley said Crue would think that me staying in Texas had something to do with him. But he'd be wrong. Crue didn't factor into my decision at all, and I was proud of that. Staying here was my choice, and it was the right move for all parties involved. Crue may haunt the edges of my mind, but he didn't affect me the way he once did.

After we broke up, he'd begged and pleaded with me to take him back. To forgive him. And I guess somewhere along the way, I had. To a certain extent, I even understood that he thought he was doing the right thing when he'd cheated on me. That he was trying to protect Cash and me. But the trust we once had was lost, and without it, we weren't possible.

"In order for me to love you the way you want to be loved, I need you to trust me."

"I do trust you."

Sort of hiding, I was in my childhood room, sitting on my bed with my laptop balanced on my knees. I was reworking the MJ Botanicals website. There was something I didn't love about the page headers. The spacing was off.

"I saw Colin leaving with a packed suitcase and no girlfriend." I glanced up. Cash was leaning in my doorway, backward baseball cap on his head, and hands shoved in his pockets.

"I set him free."

"Oregon not the place for you?" He stepped into my room, coming to sit on the edge of my bed.

I shrugged, placing my computer on my nightstand. "More like Colin isn't the guy for me." I smiled, changing the subject. "You're going to be a daddy."

"I am." His face lit up like a Christmas tree. "I used to make fun of how the Devil's Share popped out babies like rabbits, but now I'm adding to the herd."

"That's life, right? You grow up, fall in love, have some kids, and then grow old as shit." I was still working on the fall in love aspect of it all. Maybe I never would, maybe I'd be everyone's fun aunt until I was old and gray. Katie and Kasen had a hot as hell older uncle, he was single and seemed happy enough. "Me, Jett, Evie, and Crue are the only ones holding out in the babies department."

"Actually, I'm shocked Jett hasn't knocked up Devin yet. His master bedroom is made of fucking glass windows. I can actually see how often they bang." I wrinkled my nose and he nodded in agreement. "And as far as Crue goes, he'll never settle down. This girl broke his heart when we were kids and he's never recovered."

"Harsh." I shoved his shoulder. "He broke mine first." I knew Cash was mostly kidding, but I also knew he loved his twin a whole hell of a lot. "I'm sure he'll get some one-night stand pregnant and end up thriving with that weekend dad life."

"And you? You want babies one day?"

"Do you want babies?"

"Yes."

"Then I'll give them to you, baby."

Why in the holy hell were all these past conversations flying through my mind like a bad flashback reel? That was the third freaking time in the last ten minutes. Did breaking up with Colin damage my psyche? I wasn't harboring some long-lost feelings for fucking Crue Matthews. That asshole.

"Avory?"

"Huh? Oh. Um, yeah I want kids." I got to my feet. I needed some fresh air to clear my foggy brain. "Maybe I'll adopt one day. Who knows, right?" I held my hand out, dragging Cash to his feet. "Come on, let me walk you home."

Chapter Eight

Crue

Now

I was sitting in the moonlight, drinking vodka from a flask. It wasn't one of my finest moments, but it also wasn't my lowest. My ears had perked up a few minutes ago, the sound of someone moving through the tall grass breaking the silence of the night. I figured it was Cash coming to check on me, or maybe even Brody. I hoped it was Brody. He'd bring weed and his peaceful energy. Plus, he was happy to not talk shit out, whereas Cash would demand we unpack what I was feeling.

Avory's long dark hair came into view, shocking me speechless. I opened my mouth, then closed it again because I wasn't sure what the hell to say. Because I was me, I went with self-assured sarcasm moments later. "Just like old times?"

She jumped, her hands flying to her chest. "Holy shit, Crue, you scared me." She took a few deep breaths, then kicked a rock with the toe of her boot. "Why are you lurking in the shadows like that?"

"Why are you sneaking off the compound in the middle of the night like you're sixteen again?" My tone sounded hopeful, even to my own ears. Was she looking for me? We were standing near the back gate, the place where I first kissed her within feet from where we now stood. This was my safe place, but it was hers too. I'd been happy to share it with her. And she'd come here tonight of all nights.

It meant something, right?

"I needed to talk to you, you weren't home, so I figured…" She glanced around the field, her gaze lingering on the old chair that was still there. It had to be made of magic, holding up to the years and the elements.

"Jett already told me." I couldn't stand to hear her say the words, to say she was leaving me out loud. Because that's what it would be. If Avory left Texas, she'd be leaving me, I knew that. I lived here in the old red barn. I worked for both family companies, arranging our security details and transports. I was tied to this compound, like she had been.

"I can't wait to leave here, to leave this place."

I chuckled, tangling my fingers into her dark locks and tugging from the base the way she liked. "You want to peel out of here and never look back, baby?" I knew she didn't. I knew that she'd start to miss our loud crazy family the second we left.

"Okay, fine." She turned in my lap, straddling me in the old chair by the back gate. "How 'bout I can't wait to be free of my parents' house?"

"You and me both." I rested my palms on her toned thighs, leaning my head back so I could look at my beautiful girl in the moonlight.

"I want to build a house down here, closer to the back gate, closer to our place." She glanced around, taking in the dark field all around us.

I knew she'd want to live here forever, even though she complained constantly about all the people, the parents, and the chaos. Avory loved her family, and she loved this land. We'd both been running free across these acres from the moment we'd learned to walk. We were born wild. We were born different from our siblings, but we were still Devil's Spawn at heart, and leaving would never feel all the way right.

"I'll build you a house back here, baby. Back here where no one can hear you screaming my name."

"Crue, are you listening to me? I wanted to tell you—"

"I know you do." I cleared the fog from my brain, pushing the memory of her in my arms to the dark corners of my mind. "But I don't want to hear it, Avory. I don't want to hear about your perfect fucking boyfriend and the life you're going to live together." I shook my head. "I can't."

Chapter Nine

Avory

Now

I can't. The sadness I heard in Crue's voice should have made me feel empathy, should have made me put him out of his misery. I should have told my first love the truth: that I wasn't leaving, that I broke up with Colin. But instead, his agony made me lie.

"He's a nice guy." He closed his eyes at my soft declaration, like maybe if he didn't look at me, my words wouldn't cut so deep. "He loves me, Crue." I couldn't have him thinking I stayed because of him. I couldn't. If he thought there was a chance, he'd never let me go. And he'd already held on too long. "He'll never hurt me."

His eyes flew open, the pain in them clear as day even in the dark night. He nodded, his jaw clenched tight. "He's a nice guy, and he loves you, we can all see that." He was agreeing with me, but I knew that tone of his. He was leading me somewhere, he was luring me into a trap.

"He'll never hurt me." I punctuated the urgency in my voice by stepping closer, the dry grass crunching under my feet. Crue hurt me, and I was throwing it back in his face. I was trying to make him see that we were no good for each other, that the damage was done and we were forever over.

He scoffed. "Of course he won't hurt you, Avory." He handed me the flask in his hand, watching silently as I took an appreciative sip. "He doesn't have the capability."

I handed it back, our fingers touching for the briefest moment. "What the hell is that supposed to mean?"

His gaze traveled off, like I was starting to bore him. "You aren't in love with him. He doesn't own your heart. You can't break what you don't possess, baby spawn."

I wasn't in love with Colin, not anymore. But Crue didn't know that. I was standing here lying out my ass, telling him that Colin was the guy for me, that I was choosing him, and Crue was calling me on it. Did he still know me that well, even after all these years? Or. Had I become a shit liar in my feeble attempt to be a better person? "I *do* love him."

"You *like* him."

I couldn't back down. And I had no fucking clue why. "He makes me laugh."

"So does Jett."

"He makes me happy, Crue." I was lying and he was challenging me. He was pushing me, like he used to. Crue and I loved in a way that wouldn't make sense to anyone else. He was an asshole and I was a brat, and we fucking craved that from each other.

"I'm glad. You deserve happiness, Avory." He took another sip off the silver flask he'd had since we were kids.

"That flask is like your security blanket." I took it from his hands, tipping it back and draining the small amount of vodka that was left.

"You're right." He shoved it into his back pocket when I passed it to him, his eyes searching the party raging in front of us. "Because right now, it's the only thing keeping me calm."

"They don't matter." Three of his teammates had asked me out this week, and one of them was staring at me from across the empty pasture. Crue was jealous and possessive. The fact he couldn't beat the ever-loving shit out of those guys for looking at me made him twitchy.

"That you're trying to kill them with your mind like a fucking Jedi isn't helping any of us keep your secrets." Cash was sitting on the other side of me, adding to the pretense that we were simply three inseparable Spawn.

Crue hopped down from his tailgate, standing in front of his twin but speaking to me. I looked over his shoulder, adding to the illusion we worked so hard to maintain. "I'm going to drive you out to the middle of nowhere, lay you out under the stars and fuck you until you can't remember your own name, let alone theirs." He jerked his thumb behind him, the wicked smile on his handsome face making my blood start to heat inside my veins.

"Already forgotten, but okay." I stood up, resting my hands on Cash's shoulders and pulling him back so he'd look up at me. "Take me home, C Money?"

He sighed, scrubbing his hands down his face. "Of course." He hated the lies, but he loved us more. "See you later, bro?"

Crue nodded, pulling his cell out of his back pocket and speaking loudly. "Yeah, I'll catch up with you two later." He glanced up, winking at me as Cash helped me down.

Yeah. Crue had always had that flask. And he'd always needed it when it came to dealing with me.

Chapter Ten

Crue

Now

I wasn't being an asshole. Well, okay, I was. But I was also being myself. I was being the guy Avory fell in love with all those years ago. I'd never coddled her. I'd never bowed to her whims. I challenged her, and she challenged me right back. When we broke up, she put distance between us, her anger simmering from afar. But I needed that hate to blaze in my face. I needed that spark left between us to ignite. I needed to make her burn for me, the way she used to.

Her chin lifted defiantly, highlighting her sharp jawline. "I'm moving to Portland."

I closed the small gap left between us. "See, that's where you're wrong." I pointed back in the direction of her childhood home. "That nice guy, sleeping peacefully in your parents' guest room because he oozes respect, he isn't the guy for you. You're reaching. You're playing it safe. You're trying to be someone you're not. Nice isn't what you want, and we both know it."

"Maybe I've changed. Maybe I like nice. Maybe I *love* nice."

"I know exactly what you love, Avory."

"No you don't. You know *nothing* about me." She was staring up at me, the fire I craved burning hot in her beautiful eyes. She was pissed. But she was also turned on. She was gearing up for a fight, begging to be put in her place. No, that tech dude would never be what she needed. If he was, she wouldn't be daring me with that gaze of hers. The heat was missing between them, and she was seeking out my warmth like she was encased in ice.

"Go home, baby spawn, before I wrap my hand around that pretty throat of yours and prove you wrong."

She put both her hands on my chest, using all her strength to try to shove me back. "Fuck you, Crue." She shoved again and again, until she was out of breath and panting. "I fucking hate you." She shoved me one more time and knocked the flask out of my hand before turning away.

"There's a real fine line between love and hate, baby." I watched her stomp through the tall grass, tracking her movements until she was on the safety of the gravel road that wound around the compound.

I'd spent the last five years giving Avory space, giving her the time she needed to see that we were end game. I stayed on the edges of her life waiting for her to forgive me. I didn't care that she dated, or at least, I didn't openly care. But that guy? I'd be damned if I let him move my girl across the fucking country. He wasn't the guy for her anyway. He was safe and boring, and he treated her like she was a porcelain doll, doting on her and giving her her way every chance he got.

But my girl didn't like to be loved like that.

"Harder."

I looked up at the gorgeous girl on her knees above me. Her head was thrown back and she was riding my hand, her nails digging into my shoulders. We'd started out the night watching a movie in my parents' media room. But that hadn't lasted long.

"Crue, harder."

I wrapped my free arm around her small waist, flipping us over and laying her out on the ground. "You are the hottest fucking thing I've ever seen." I threaded my fingers in her hair, tugging her head back, exposing her throat. I kissed her flesh, licking my way up to her ear. "You remember the safe word, baby?"

She nodded, and I added a third finger inside her tight pussy, giving her exactly what she was demanding. What she was always demanding from me. More. Harder. I had to work my ass off to be enough for my girl, and I fucking loved it.

No. That guy she claimed to love would never be enough for her.

She wouldn't be happy with him, and she wouldn't leave with him.

She couldn't.

Chapter Eleven

Avory

Now

"I did something bad." I was pacing in Jett's office. It was after midnight and luckily he and Marley had both been up at MJ Botanicals. When I left Crue by the back gate, I'd immediately run across the compound, searching out someone to confide in. They had a conference call with an overseas company and the time change was working in my favor.

Jett held his hand over his mouth, stifling a yawn. "You mean other than break up with that super-nice guy?"

Marley's eyebrows rose to her dark hairline. "You dumped Colin already?" She shuffled some papers on the desk and closed her laptop. "I figured you'd at least wait until you guys got back to Austin."

Shit. Should I have waited? Once I'd made up my mind, I couldn't seem to take another minute to end things. Ugh. I was a selfish brat. I broke up with him at my parents' house and he'd had to pack and leave in front of them. I was the worst. But that wasn't the current issue at hand.

"I just lied to Crue." I was pacing, and my watch vibrated on my wrist, telling me I'd met my activity challenge for the day. "I told him that I was going to Portland with Colin. I told him that I was in love and happy, and moving."

"What the hell for?" Jett kicked his feet up on his desk, knocking over a thankfully empty coffee mug. I originally came to talk to Marley, my sounding board of a baby sister. But Jett was good with advice too. He didn't sugarcoat things, but he tried to soften the inevitable blow.

"At first, I was trying to help Crue. I thought maybe if he thought I was leaving, he'd finally move on. But then he kept challenging me and shit. Like calling me on my feelings for Colin, and saying all this stuff about how I didn't love him and he didn't own my heart." I paused, taking a deep breath. "Which pissed me off because it kind of turned me on, you know? And I was not expecting that. I don't compare the guys I date to Crue. I swear I don't, but my fight with him highlighted what had been missing between Colin and me."

"Anger and verbal abuse? Is that what was missing between you and the tech genius?" Jett nodded, lips pursed. "Makes tons of sense."

"It's not anger, or abuse. It's, uh, I don't know, it's—"

"Passion." Marley sighed, like we were all stupid and she was tired of dealing with our ineptitude. "You and Crue, your passion is tied up in the way you two don't back down. You get off on it. You were so young, so impressionable when you fell in love. You don't know any other way."

I'd never thought of it like that before. I was only fifteen when Crue demanded I cancel my plans before hauling into his lap, kissing me senseless. Was Marley right? Had Crue and I shaped each other so irrevocably? Were Colin and I doomed from the start because he was a nice guy and I could only fall in absolute love with assholes?

Jett pointed at Marley. "Look at MVP, putting that double minor in psychology to good use on the fucked-up people in our family." His gaze switched from her to me. "So you lied, he called bullshit, and you got wet." He waved his hand in the air, encouraging me to go on.

"So I hit him."

"Physical abuse too, huh? You two are kinkier than I thought." He sighed. "Closed fist? Backhand? How weird did this get?"

"I pushed him more than hit him, I think." I shook my head, mad at myself and mad at my first love. "He pissed me off and I reacted. I pushed him and I told him I hated him, and I can't seem to stop shaking now." I held my hands out, palms down, showing them the tremors that started as soon as I walked away and left Crue standing in the dark alone, the same way I'd found him. "Fucking Crue."

"Fuck you." I shoved his chest, hating him for flirting with another girl, even though I knew it meant nothing. "Fuck you, Crue."

"Stop." He grabbed my hands and spun me, wrapping his arms all the way around my body as I vibrated with anger. "You're being a fucking brat, Avory."

I struggled in his hold, wanting nothing more than to take all my sadness and hurt and anger out on him. He could take it. "Fuck you. I hate you. I hate this. I hate all of this."

"I know it hurts, baby." He kissed the side of my neck. "It hurts every time one of my buddies stares at your ass. It hurts every time I have to watch them ask you out. It hurts when I have to listen to those chicks whisper shit into my ears. It all hurts, Avory." He overpowered me, picking me up and sitting down with me in his lap, his arms clamped tight. "But it's all worth it, because at the end of the day, it's you and me. All the crap we go through fades away as soon as we're alone."

"I fucking hate you." I was crying, all the power behind my anger gone. It was like he'd siphoned all my frustration, pulling it into his body.

"You don't." He kissed my neck again, one of his hands threading into my hair. "You love me, baby." He tugged my head back, fusing his lips to mine. "And I love you. I love you so fucking much."

"Do you want to be with Crue? Is this what this is actually about?" Jett was standing now and staring at me as I tried to shake the unwanted memories from my mind. We were explosive back then, there was no doubt about that. So maybe Marley was right, maybe we fucked each other up a long-ass time ago and neither one of us would ever be normal again.

"No." I took a deep breath, clenching my hands into fists. "I wasn't in love with Colin, not in the way he was with me. He deserved better, and I never truly wanted to go with him. But I didn't choose Crue over him." That wasn't a lie, and I was proud of my reasons for staying. Proud of myself. "I chose myself. And my family."

"Then get the hell off this compound before Crue finds out you lied to him." Marley rose as well, both of them seemingly done with me and this day. "I told you Crue would assume that you stayed because of him, and that was part of the reason you lied, we both know it."

"I was trying to help him let go, *that's* why I lied."

"You're afraid that he'll keep hanging on, and you're afraid of what you'll do if he *doesn't* let go." Marley cut me off at the knees, laying the truths out there that I didn't even know existed.

"I don't love him anymore." I didn't. I'd moved on so very long ago. He'd hurt me and I'd ended things. From that moment on I didn't let Crue control me. I didn't let myself miss him. Hell, until recently I never really even let myself think of him. These memories that kept flooding my mind were new, and incredibly inconvenient.

Jett snorted, putting his hands on my shoulders to lead me down the hallway toward the front entrance. "Then you really shouldn't have felt the need to lie."

Chapter Twelve

Crue

Three days. That's how long I'd been holed up in the old red barn. I'd spent the weekend drinking and slipping back into the despair I'd felt when Avory broke up with me. She was leaving. *Fuck.* She was choosing Colin. She was making a mistake. She didn't love him, not really. But how was I supposed to make her see that? If I pushed, would she push back? If I demanded her attention, would that only drive her away faster? I was so unsure of my next move and it was pissing me the hell off.

I knew she still felt something for me. I knew it. I'd witnessed the spark that remained between us the other night by the back gate. She'd been angry, she'd yelled and shoved me. She'd raged against my body the way she had when we were young.

But that was days ago. And I'd been too chickenshit to venture outside of this former grow house ever since. I was terrified that she'd still be here. I was terrified that she'd be gone. I was afraid that my family would be talking about how happy they were for her. I was afraid my aunts would be planning a going away party. I was being ruled by fear and uncertainty, and it felt as pathetic as it fucking sounded.

That wasn't me. Not anymore. I needed to get my shit together so I didn't become the worst version of myself all over again. Losing Avory would be painful, but letting her slip away without a fight would be crippling.

"Well, look who decided to grace us with his presence." Jett leaned back in his black leather desk chair, grinning as I tossed him the contracts for the private plan bringing his newest round of investors into Austin later in the week. He was being dramatic. I'd only neglected to come into the office on Monday.

"I've got to get to work on the RiffRaff tour schedules for next year, so unless you need anything else, I'm headed to my other job." I had two, one here at MJ Botanicals and one in Austin at RiffRaff Records' head office.

"You're going to Austin today?" Jett pulled an envelope from his desk drawer with Avory's name written in thick red sharpie across the top. "Can you drop this at Avory's loft? It'll save me the cost of a courier. Thanks." He turned back to his computer, like he hadn't handed me a smoking bomb.

"I'll pay the cost of the courier." I dropped it back on top of the contracts I'd given him. "I'm not going to Avory's." I'd never been to her town house, and I sure as fuck didn't want to head there now to watch her pack.

"Oh okay." He picked the envelope up and put it in the drawer it'd come from. "I thought maybe you'd be going there to tell her bye at some point or something. But no big deal if you can't handle it. I'll get it sent over this afternoon."

"Can't handle it? What's that supposed to mean?" I couldn't, but he sure as fuck didn't need to know that.

"Look, I get it, Crue." He held his hands up. "I wouldn't want to see my first love packing up her place to move across the country to be with another guy either." He hit his chest with the side of his fist. "That would be like a knife to the chest."

Was he reading my mind? Or was I being that fucking predictable? Either way, I didn't like it.

"What are you talking about? I thought Avory broke up with Colin this weekend?" Talon walked into the office, talking around the apple he was eating, giving me more hope than I'd had since I was eighteen and had ruined everything good in my life.

"What?" I stepped closer to the blond germaphobe, barely resisting the urge to grab him by the shirt collar. "Avory broke up with him? When?"

"Uh, Marley said Avory wasn't moving to Portland." Talon's eyes jerked from me to Jett, like he was unsure of what he'd stepped into.

I narrowed my gaze on Jett, towering over him, daring him to lie to me. "What the hell is going on?"

"You are the actual worst, you know that?" Jett sighed, shaking his head at Talon.

Talon jerked back. "What the fuck did I do now?"

"I wanted Crue to storm into Avory's apartment and demand she stay, make this big speech or gesture or whatever. And then he'd see that she wasn't packing and that Colin's stuff was gone." Jett threw his hands in the air. "It was going to be this epic moment and you fucking ruined it."

Talon rolled his eyes, throwing his apple core at Jett. "You're the most dramatic dude I've ever met."

I ignored their typical back and forth, focusing on the important issue instead. "She lied to me?" Avory fucking lied to me, and then slapped the shit out of me when I called her on it? I *knew* she wouldn't leave. I *knew* she didn't love him. "Why? Why would she lie?"

"Go ask her." Jett pulled the manila envelope back out of his desk, launching it to me like a Frisbee.

Chapter Thirteen

Crue

Now

I held the envelope with Avory's name on it in front of me like a shield as proof I had a valid reason to see her. *Hey, it wasn't my idea. I'm doing Jett a favor.*

I knocked on the white door, listening intently, praying I didn't hear Colin's voice. Maybe Talon had been wrong. Maybe they'd gotten back together. Maybe she'd open the door and all I'd see were stacks and stacks of brown boxes stuffed with her life inside.

"Crue?" She must have looked through the peephole because she said my name before she even opened the door all the way. "What are you doing here?" She was wearing tight leggings with a black camo pattern and a black sports bra. Her hair was down and hanging to her waist, and her pouty lips were painted a cherry red. She always looked like she'd stepped off a shoot for *Playboy*. And no matter how much time went by, my dick always hardened at the mere sight of her.

I held up the envelope, working to clear the instant lust from my voice. "Jett asked me to drop this off on my way to RiffRaff." I handed it to her and then stepped past her into her loft. I'd never been here before. She'd never invited me, and I'd never felt the urge to barge in until today.

Rich caramel leather couches sat on a vibrant vintage area rug. Between the couches was a glass coffee table edged in brass, which reflected the enlarged photographs hanging on the walls I recognized from her mom's old photo albums: spilled liquor bottles, and broken glass. They were images from the first tour Aunt Lex went on with the Devil's Share. *I'd been so right about Avory.* This girl, my girl, would never leave her family. No matter how much everyone annoyed her, no matter how irritated she pretended to be, she loved every single one of us.

"This envelope is empty, Crue." I turned around to see her standing by the front door, the package upside down. "Did Jett send you over here as a joke? Or did you lie to me so I'd open the door and let you in?"

Fucking Jett. I was going to wring his meddling little neck the next time I saw him.

I scoffed, not answering either of her questions. "If we're going to start talking about lies, how 'bout we start with the ones you told me the other night?"

Avory crossed her arms over her chest, drawing my attention there, her hip jutted out to the side. Instant fucking attitude like always. "I was trying to do you a favor."

I raised an eyebrow, stepping closer, catching the scent of her shampoo, which smelled like high school and warm summer nights. "Doing me a favor? How the hell do you figure?"

"You need to let this fantasy of us go, and I thought if you assumed I was leaving with Colin that maybe you'd finally be able to get over me." She sighed, like she was bored with our conversation.

Her words cut, but I couldn't let her know she wasn't wrong. I wasn't over her, and I probably should let go of the fantasy of us ending up together. But then again... "I'll let it go when you do, baby spawn."

"I've moved on, Crue."

I chuckled. "Have you? Because the last time we spoke, I was under your skin. I got a big glimpse of that girl I used to know. The one who used to come on my dick and then instantly beg for more." I was goading her, and I was being an asshole. But that was the only way I'd gotten a reaction out of her a few nights ago. I was living on a wing and a prayer, hoping it would work again.

Avory shuffled her feet, letting me know she was uncomfortable with this conversation. "You're so fucking full of yourself. It's disgusting." She had the same tells she always had.

Avory shuffled her feet, lying to her dad about her plans for the night. "I'm going to a friend's house after the game, but I'll be home by curfew."

I longed for the day that we didn't have to lie to our parents. "I can pick her up on my way home." I slung an arm around her shoulders, playing the part of her older protective cousin. "I'll make sure she's back before curfew, Uncle Dash." And she would be. We'd be at the back of the compound, naked and on a blanket underneath the stars.

"All right, you two, you have fun."

I opened my car door as her dad walked off, helping her inside the cab of my truck. When I climbed into the driver's seat, she pulled up the middle console and had her mouth wrapped around my dick before we were even out of the school parking lot. My girl was a fucking dream come true and I was the luckiest bastard in the world.

"Crue? Are you even fucking listening to me?" Avory stepped forward, snapping her sassy fingers in front of my face. "I moved on a long time ago, and it's really time you do the same."

I didn't believe her. I never had. I'd hurt her. She'd dumped me, and then spent the next several years making me pay penance for my actions. But when she'd had an out, a way to live her life away from me and the compound where we'd fallen in love, she'd turned it down. And she could say that I didn't factor into that choice until she was blue in the face, but we both knew it was a damn lie. She was here, in front of me, single and laid bare. It was time I reclaimed the girl that had always been mine.

"No."

Her doe eyes went wide. "Excuse me?"

"There's still something there between us, and you know it. It's the reason you lied to me about moving, and it's the same reason you lost your shit when I called you on your feelings for Colin. It's the reason you pushed me. It's the reason you walked away."

I closed the gap between us. "We're explosive, you and I. We always have been, baby spawn. There will never be another man who can love you the way I can, the way I *do*. Colin sure as fuck couldn't." I threaded my fingers through her hair, tugging close to her scalp the way she liked. "I'm done giving you your space. I'm done letting you punish me for breaking us. You've been throwing a temper tantrum for half a fucking decade. And now it's time to grow up, little girl." I loosened my grip, letting her long locks fall through my fingers.

"Get the hell out." Her eyes were hard, fire building in their depths. She stepped to the side, pointed to the still-open front door. "Now."

I watched her for a few moments, taking my time while pissing her off even more. I was done catering to her wishes, to her heartache. I was hurting too. Had been for years. It took two of us to fall in love and two of us to destroy what we had. It was time I reminded her of that. I was done letting Avory Connor run my life. Run our life, our future.

"See you around, baby spawn." I placed a kiss on the corner of her mouth, riling her up on my way out the door.

Chapter Fourteen

Avory

Now

Marley's assessment of Crue and me stuck in my head all night. I'd still been thinking about it when he'd showed up at my house a few mornings later. And then he'd said the same thing: that we were explosive and the fire between us was still burning. I threw him out and he'd had the audacity to kiss me before he left.

I'd be damned if I didn't feel that kiss all the way down to the depths of my soul. And now I was at my parents' house for dinner, still fucking thinking about it all. Which I'd say was a little inappropriate, but Crue and I had done so many other *inappropriate* things at my parents' dinner table.

I bit my lip, trying like hell to keep silent while Crue's fingers inched their way up my bare thigh. I was wearing my cheerleading outfit, there was a football game tonight. I spread my legs wider, making room for him to do what he pleased.

"Crue, two-a-days start soon, baseball season is right around the corner."

Crue let out a low appreciative hum and he flicked my clit through my damp panties. "I'm so ready."

I clenched my teeth, not wanting my wicked smile to give us away either. Crue was ready for something, but it wasn't baseball season.

"Baby girl, you're going to have to start driving yourself to school, Crue and Cash will have morning practice." I should be ashamed of myself, but my father's concern mixed with Crue's wandering hands made me feel like a live wire.

"Nah, I'll take care of her." Crue moved my panties to the side.

My dad smiled, resting his chin on his fist. "I suppose you could get in some extra study time before school."

I nodded, my cheeks flushed. I couldn't open my mouth to speak, a moan would come out instead.

"You kids have plans tonight?"

I couldn't answer, so I nodded and Crue grinned.

I'd cheered at the game, and then Crue brought me home. We'd stopped in the kitchen to have a snack before we headed out to yet another field party, but then my dad spotted us. He sat at the table and immediately started talking baseball.

"We were going to head out to a party." Crue moved his fingers lower, teasing my entrance. "But it's getting late, and I don't want Avory to miss curfew. Maybe we should just stay here and watch a movie?" He glanced at me, humor and lust evident in his eyes.

"Lex and I were thinking about watching one too, we'll join you." He got up from the table. "I'll pop some popcorn."

Crue grinned. "Sounds perfect."

The second my dad was out of sight I dropped my forehead to the table. "A movie with my parents? Really?"

Crue moved his hand away, licking his fingers clean. "Really." He leaned down, whispering in my ear. "We'll get a blanket, turn off the lights...it'll be fun, baby spawn."

I cleared my throat, and that vivid memory from my mind. Crue was right. Marley was right. I was fucked up, and I'd never be able to fall in love with a nice guy. I wanted to blame Crue. I wanted to believe that he did this to me, that he made me this way. But that wasn't fair, and was historically inaccurate. I'd craved everything he did to me, always eager for more.

"I always liked it like that." Shit, I said that out loud sitting with my poor perpetually out-of-the-loop parents.

"What?"

My eyes went wide, my breath caught in my chest. "Um, I always liked burnt rice." I spooned another bite into my mouth, smiling as I worked to swallow the terrible casserole my mom had made for dinner. "So good, Mom." I even gave a thumbs-up to really sell it.

"Liar." My dad coughed into his napkin, spitting some food in there. "You want to tell us what happened with Colin?"

My parents had asked me to come to dinner, and I knew they were fishing for information about my breakup. I hadn't given them any details after Colin left, and they hadn't pushed. But it'd been a week and now they wanted answers. I couldn't blame them.

I moved the dry chicken breast around on my plate, trying to hide it under the doughy roll I couldn't choke down. "I didn't want to move to Portland, and I refused to let him pass up that job offer to stay in Austin with me."

"You could have tried long distance. Did he not want that?" My mom set her plate on the floor, allowing our newest rescue mutt to finish her dinner. But even she didn't like to eat the food Mom cooked.

"He wanted to stay, or was fine trying long distance. He wanted to make our relationship work." I nodded, taking a small sip of my wine. "It was me. I wasn't in love with him, not like he was in love with me. He deserved more."

"I'm sorry, sweetheart." My dad reached across the table, resting his hand on top of mine. "He's a nice guy."

He was too nice. Apparently, that was the problem. I needed someone to call me a brat and pull my hair in order to fall in love. "He is, and I'm sure he'll find someone who will appreciate that about him."

I smiled at them, letting them know that I was going to be okay.

***

After my third glass of wine, my parents had insisted that I stay the night. So, here I was in my childhood bedroom, snuggled under the covers. Even though my sisters lived within walking distance, my mom got giddy when we slept at home. Last year for her birthday, Halen, Marley, and I all stayed at our parents' house for a night. We'd eaten dinner together and watched movies piled on the couch. My mom cried tears of joy when she caught us up giggling at two o'clock in the morning.

How could I ever think, even for a minute, that I would survive leaving this town? This was where I learned to walk, learned to run. I got stitches after I cut my foot on a rock down by the tank. I'd been chasing Crue and Cash. We were maybe seven and eight? Cash carried me all the way back to my house. Crue? Well, he'd saved the rock, and after I got home from the hospital he'd handed me a hammer and told me to destroy the things that hurt me.

Who knew that ten years later, he'd be the one to hurt me? Think I didn't conjure visions of using that same hammer on him? Think again.

My phone vibrated on the nightstand. It was late but all my friends from college hadn't gotten big-girl jobs like I had. I figured it was an invite downtown, so when I saw Crue's name flash across my screen, I almost dropped my fucking phone.

Crue: You lost your virginity in that bed.

What the hell? Was he spying on me? I closed my eyes, taking a deep calming breath. After I'd broken up with him, Crue had crawled into a hole like a wounded animal. So why now? Why was he pushing me so hard now after all this time? After all the guys I've paraded in front of him? After all the years apart?

Avory: I got a new bed after we broke up.

Crue: When did you become such a liar?

Avory: Around the time you became so fucking delusional.

I smiled, proud of myself for that comeback.

Crue: Your window locked, baby spawn?

Avory: Bolted shut.

Crue Matthews hadn't texted me in years. Like actual years. I was annoyed, but a little intrigued. I didn't understand what his end game was. I didn't know what he was after. Did he want to prove that I still wanted him? That he still had the power to make me weak in the knees? Of course he did. No one had ever made me feel the way Crue did when we were kids. He'd been my first love, my first everything. My first heartbreak. My first devastation too.

Crue: I'm sorry about Colin.

Avory: Now who is the liar?

Crue: I don't ever want to see you hurt Avory. So I am truly sorry if breaking up with him hurt you.

That was sweet. Which pissed me off. I didn't need him to be nice to me. I didn't need him to care about my feelings. Fuck him.

Avory: I'm made of tougher stuff than that. A boy broke my heart when I was a kid. Nothing could ever hurt as much as that did.

There, asshole. We aren't friends, we're barely family at this point. I didn't need him texting me in the middle of the night. I didn't need him dropping by my condo. I didn't want him to think of me, and I sure as shit didn't want to think of him. Ever. I should have fucking moved to Portland, if only to get away from him.

Crue: Stupid boy.

Avory: Agreed. Now stop texting me. It's weird.

Crue: You used to love it when I'd text you at night. I'd wait until you were in bed. I'd demand you touch yourself, tell you exactly what to do with those talented little fingers of yours. Remember that?

How could I forget? And I'd been so eager to please him, so eager to follow his instructions. He'd make me tease myself until he could sneak out of his house and into my window. My stomach dipped thinking about those nights. I rubbed my thighs together, hating my body's reaction to him.

I should have ignored him. I should have shut off my phone. But that wasn't who I was, and we both knew it. If Crue wanted to play this odd little game, fucking fine by me. He'd lose.

Avory: I do remember that. I remember everything.

Crue: Tell me what else you remember, baby.

Avory: I remember the baseball dugout before that big playoff game for regionals when I accidentally left my panties behind, and you found them, put them in your pocket, and then hit that game-winning home run.

Crue: Best good luck charm ever.

Avory: I remember the time we went skinny-dipping in the lake, swimming off into the dark while that party got crazy around us. I screamed so loud it scared those ducks.

Crue: We had to walk the long way back around. I carried you and everyone kept asking why my back was all wet.

Avory: Our first kiss, down by the back gate. I'd never been kissed like that before. It felt like all my nerve endings were firing at once.

Crue: Nothing had ever felt so good, so real.

I was leading him somewhere, using his own tactics against him. I wanted to hurt him. But in the process I was hurting myself. I didn't think I'd care. I didn't think these memories mattered to me at all. But as I typed, I started to cry. My heart broke all over again for those kids we used to be. My god, we were so in love. So completely enamored with each other. Until we weren't.

Avory: How about that time we were at family dinner and Uncle Smith showed everyone the pictures of you cheating on me?

Crue: Avory.

Avory: Remember that? I had to smile and pretend like I wasn't dying inside. I bit my cheek to keep from crying. I bit it so hard that I bled.

Crue: I did it to save you, to save Cash. And you know that.

Avory: Leave me alone, Crue. We aren't those kids anymore. There's no use remembering the good times because the bad ones always creep in.

Crue: Only when you let them.

I wiped at my eyes, refusing to let one more tear fall for Crue Matthews. Maybe he had been trying to save me. Maybe he had been trying to save Cash. But that didn't make it okay, and it didn't change history. He cheated, and he broke my trust. Without trust, we had nothing.

Chapter Fifteen

Crue

Now

Avory was fucking tough as nails, she always had been. Last night I'd tried to drag up some nostalgia and she'd handed me my ass on a silver fucking platter. I should have known she was leading me somewhere. I should have known she wouldn't make it that easy for me.

"Yo, you decent?" Cash and Katie walked into my front door, not bothering to knock.

I took another pull from the beer I was nursing on my couch, completely clothed. "And if I hadn't been?"

"I've seen your, uh, stuff more times than I'd care to admit." Katie sat next to me, stealing the bag of chips I'd been eating for lunch. "I can't even count the number of times I had to help Cash get your drunk ass into bed."

Katie and Cash had taken care of me at a time in my life when I'd basically wanted to die. I'd moved to Cali with my brother after we graduated because staying here wasn't an option. I told Avory I was going to go to the University of Texas and live at home until her senior year was over. She told me if I did that she'd have her parents send her to a boarding school in Switzerland.

"I heard Avory isn't moving to Portland." Cash kicked his feet up on my coffee table, resting one hand on his wife's knee.

"Did she tell you that? Or did she lie to your fucking face too?"

"She lied to you?" Katie spoke around a mouthful of chips. "Why?"

"Should you be eating that much salt?" I took the bag away from her, holding it high out of her reach when she made a grab for it.

"You know, I used to think it was sweet that all of you guys were so involved with the females in this family. You go to doctors' appointments and babysit while people are on bed rest. Joined in pregnancy yoga and made sure they stayed hydrated. But now that I'm the one knocked up, I find the lot of you incredibly annoying." Katie stood, glaring at me on her way into the kitchen.

"There are some strawberries in the fridge." I chuckled when she shot me the bird behind her back.

"Avory lied to you about leaving?" Cash seemed content to let Katie and me fight it out, as always. "Why?"

"I asked her the same question, and she told me it was for my own good. She said I needed to move on, and she figured if I thought she was going with Colin, I'd give up on *us*."

Cash winced. "Brutal."

"I think she lied because she's scared." I'd thought about it a lot over the last few days. "She didn't want to leave, and part of that had to do with me." It *had* to. Like, it fucking had to or everything I was trying to accomplish getting her back was for nothing.

"Why do you think you factor into her decisions after all this time?" Katie asked while walking in with a bowl of strawberries.

"I feel like pregnancy has given you a bit of an edge." Katie was the nicest person on the planet, and hearing her spout harsh realities was bumming me out. Like kicking a dog when he was already pretty fucking low down.

"It's an honest question. What makes you think you still matter that much? I want to know."

I glanced at Cash and he shrugged, letting me know he was curious as well. I sighed, trying to put how I was feeling into words. "The love I had with Avory, it was so fucking deep. The way we loved each other, I can't ever imagine someone else being able to measure up. For either of us." I took another sip of my beer before continuing. "I broke her trust, and trust with us was everything. I deserved her anger, so instead of pushing her, I ran off to Cali with you guys."

"You think things would have been different if you'd have stayed here in Texas?" Cash was rubbing his palm on Katie's tiny bump. "If you'd have stayed in her life, in her face?"

"Maybe." Or my presence could have pissed her off enough to do something rash and stupid. There was no way of knowing what might have been, and dwelling on it could drive a sane man crazy. "Either way, I'm here now, and I'm done letting her throw a fit about something that happened five years ago."

"You cheated on her." Cash sounded wary, like he wasn't sure I remember what I'd done. "Saying 'something that happened' sounds like you're making it less than it was."

I gritted my teeth, so fucking tired of having to defend myself. "I went on a date to save her ass and yours. That chick had intel. Names, places, she had it all. I was going to tell Avory as soon as I got home, but then that bitch crawled into my lap and took off her shirt." My stomach churned at the memory. "When I got home, I showered twice and smoked myself to sleep."

"So it was really just a kiss." Cash sounded relieved.

My jaw dropped at his statement. "Have you gone the last five fucking years thinking I slept with that whore? Are you serious? Why didn't you fucking ask me?" I couldn't imagine spending half a decade thinking my twin was capable of something so skeevy.

"I mean, I don't know. I guess you were already so messed up over the whole thing, I didn't want to bring it up." Cash put his arm around Katie, kissing the side of her head. "Right after it happened I boarded a plane to Europe, and by the time we got home, you seemed so closed off, scarred."

"*She* kissed me. I kissed her back because she said if I didn't she'd name names and tell the girls we switched on what happened." I swallowed thickly, recalling how hopeless I'd felt in that moment. "After she took her shirt off, I shoved her off me and took her ass home."

"You cheated, but you had your reasons, and they were all pretty damn selfless," Katie said between strawberries. "You were trying to keep your relationship with Avory under wraps so you could keep seeing her. And you were trying to right the wrong you inflicted on your brother." Katie turned in her seat, meeting my eyes. "A wrong, I might add, that Avory was all for. Did she ever protest? Did she ever put anyone else's needs before her own? Of course not. Avory is no angel, and it's about fucking time all of you see that."

Katie polished off the last strawberry and then licked her fingers. "She was a spoiled brat who wanted her way no matter who got hurt." Katie used her thumb to gesture at Cash. "You were both in the wrong, but you," she pointed at Crue, "you're the only one who has owned up to their mistakes."

Chapter Sixteen

Crue

Now

I was back at MJ Botanicals. I'd like to say I didn't come here in hopes of seeing Avory, but then I'd be lying. I was finally working toward the rest of my life again, and I was like a fucking dog with a bone. I wanted Avory back in my arms, and I wanted her *now*.

"Where is everyone?"

"By everyone, do you mean Jett and Avory? The only two people who aren't here in this building of fifty employees?" Marley took off her black-framed glasses, rubbing at her pretty eyes when I strolled into her office.

"Yes." There was no use denying it, she'd only continue to call me on my bullshit. Marley didn't play games, and she sure as hell didn't put up with stupid petty lies. I'd been a lot like her once upon a time. Maybe I wasn't so different from everyone in my family as I thought. Marley was a bit of an asshole, too. "Did you finally fire them for annoying you?"

She snorted. "Jett literally made me sign a contract stating that annoyance was never a reason I could dismiss an employee. Including him and Avory."

"Smart."

"I sent those two to meet with the investors we had you fly in, the ones from Ireland." She grabbed the giant coffee mug from her desk, draining every last drop before setting it back down.

Marley was a boss in every sense of the word. She was up all night with a teething baby, and running a billion-dollar corporation between nap times. "Why did you send them? Shouldn't it be *you* and Jett meeting investors?" They owned MJ Botanicals: they ran it.

They had their hands in every aspect of operating the company. I presumed huge opportunities like this one would be something Marley insisted she kept control over.

"Avory and Jett are the two most pleasingly charming people we have in this company." She shrugged. "They're like the fucking Ken and Barbie of the medical marijuana world."

"You expanding this enterprise to pimpin' out family members now?" I didn't love the idea of Avory being used for her beautiful face and banging body. And I didn't want her spending time with Irish dudes with awesome accents.

"Says the bulked-up Hemsworth clone the family uses to be the face of our security detail." She rolled her eyes, accurately pointing out that we all used each other for various reasons. "What are you doing here anyway? Stalking is a federal offense." She held up a thick packet. "Or so says the handbook Avory put on my desk this morning."

"I thought Devin was the human resources officer around here?"

"She is." Marley blinked up at me. "Avory said I needed to read up because you were, and I quote, 'suddenly up her ass.'"

"I'm not up her ass." I mean, I was showing her more attention than I had in the last five years...but I hadn't gone anywhere near that ass. Yet. "And I'm not stalking her. I work here too."

"You're contract labor, and we don't currently have anything for you to do." She tossed the papers into the trashcan. "You want to be honest with me? Or you want to leave?"

I knew Marley wasn't bluffing. If I didn't tell her the truth, she'd throw me out of her office and slam the door in my face. "I told Avory I was done letting her punish me for something that happened five years ago. She's still in love with me, and I'm not going to let her pretend like she isn't." I sighed, sitting down on the small leather loveseat. "I'm not stalking, I'm simply not going to avoid places because she might be there."

"Well, it's about time." Marley stood, going to the coffee station in the corner and pouring herself another cup. "I was wondering when you were going to put an end to Avory's epic tantrum. You've been letting her treat you like shit for the better part of a decade."

"You're not team Avory? She's your sister."

"My sister is a straight-up selfish brat most of the time, and the only person who's ever bothered to put her in her place, other than me, is you."

She wasn't wrong. Marley didn't let Avory act up, and neither did I. I loved Avory Connor, worshiped her. But I'd always refused to bow down to her moods and whims. "You think she's still in love with me?"

"I'm not answering that, she's my sister."

I scoffed. "You just said—"

"I said I agreed that she treats you like the only person who has ever fucked up in the history of this ridiculous family." She held a hand up, letting me know she wasn't finished. "We all know that's not true. Avory is no angel. But that doesn't mean I'm going to put myself in the middle of whatever is going on between the two of you."

"She didn't leave." She didn't move, she didn't choose a new life with another man.

"Doesn't mean it was because of you."

I crossed my arms over my chest. "It was partly because of me, and we all fucking know it."

"Well, there's only one thing you can do now." She sat the stainless steel coffeepot back in the warmer.

"Yeah? What's that?"

She blew on the dark black liquid, making the curling steam move closer to me. "Try to get your girl back."

Try to get your girl back. Wasn't that what I was doing? Wasn't that what I'd been doing all along? "Easier said than done."

"Don't be such a fucking pussy, Crue." Marley leaned against the edge of her desk, clutching her newest cup of coffee. She seemed to be mainlining caffeine today. "You've always been a bit of an asshole. I admired that about you, and Avory was drawn to it like a moth to a damn bonfire. Be a dick, don't back down. Be the guy she fell for, not the sap that's been paying her undue penance for the last five years."

"That really what you think? That I've been walking around with my tail tucked between my legs, waiting for Avory to forgive me?" I hurt her, and I deserved her anger. Granted, five years was a bit much.

"Yes. We all do. But I'm the only one bitchy enough to tell you to your face, pretty boy." Marley sat back behind her large messy desk. "Avory fucked up too. Your problem is you decided to stop calling her on her bullshit the day she broke up with you."

That was pretty much the same thing Katie had said the other night. Avory wasn't innocent, and it was time I stopped letting her punish me for a mistake that took two people to make. Or three if you include Cash. He should have told us to fuck off from day one.

"How did you get so smart?"

"Isn't it obvious?" I raised an eyebrow, waiting for her to tell me all her secrets. "I spent years studying all you idiots while you made your epic mistakes."

Chapter Seventeen

Avory

Now

I was back in my loft, thank god. Being at the compound was too close for comfort with Crue. I wasn't sure why all of a sudden he'd decided that we needed to be back together. It was fucking ludicrous. Did he really think I'd ever be able to trust him again? Did he really think we'd ever work after what he'd done to us?

Not a fucking chance.

And those texts last night…what the holy hell was that? I didn't want to keep taking these stupid walks down memory lane because I knew exactly where they'd lead. Right to the worst moment of my life, the moment I found out in front of my family that the guy I revered had cheated on me like it was nothing. He'd cheated. He'd pushed me away. He'd broken me.

I wiped the lone tear that decided to roll down my cheek, no doubt leaving a black trail of mascara in its wake. Crying over him after all these years. I was pathetic.

"I'm pathetic." I smiled through the waterworks still falling from my eyes. "I'm sorry."

"You never need to apologize to me." Crue wrapped his arms around my neck, drawing me in close and kissing the top of my head. "My last game means my senior year is almost over. It means soon we won't be at the same school." He pushed me back, wiping my tears with his thumbs. "I want to cry too."

"Promise nothing will change, promise you won't fall in love with an insightful English major." I knew he loved me. But he was Crue Matthews. He was temptation wrapped in a sinful package. All the girls at school lusted over him, and they weren't subtle about it.

What would happen when he was around older girls? Girls he wouldn't have to sneak around with? Girls who weren't complicated?

"Look at me, baby spawn." He held my face in his hands. "There isn't anything that could take me away from you. Anything. Anyone. I'm so fucking in love with you."

"I love you too."

"Yeah?" He smirked, wickedly handsome. "Prove it."

I couldn't help but giggle, the last of my tears vanishing in an instant. "What'd you have in mind?" In that moment I believed him, I believed that we'd be together forever because no one else would ever understand us.

"How 'bout one more round in the dugout?"

I jumped into his arms, wrapping my legs around his waist. He was already hard, knowing that I'd never turn him down. I was game. Always waiting with bated breath for the next time he'd hold me.

The sound of my cell phone ringing brought me out of the past. I needed to book an appointment with a shrink as soon as possible. These were like terrible acid flashbacks or something. Made sense. Crue had been like an addiction at one point, a drug. Either way, these memories were completely unwanted and unwarranted.

"Avory Connor." I answered my phone like a professional now. Marley insisted after a client called about a glitch with the website and I answered by saying, *What?*

"Avory, hello, this is Sean Ryan."

"Oh hello, Mr. Ryan." Jett and I had been sent to meet with these new investors, like a couple of prized ponies. It wasn't all terrible because Sean Ryan was lovely, and his accent was like music to my ears. "What can I do for you?"

"As we speak, Emmet and I are signing the contracts your office had drawn up." There was a brief pause, the sound of pen scraping against paper. Marley was old school, wanting everything in hard copy as well as digital. It drove Talon crazy because he was the most environmentally cautious person I knew. "Let's celebrate tonight when we bring them by your office, with some good Irish whiskey. How does that sound?"

Emmet and Sean Ryan were brothers from Ireland, and their family had been in the whiskey business for generations. As the two youngest, they wanted to diversify the wealth. And cannabis was the direction they'd gone. "That sounds fantastic, Mr. Ryan."

"Sean, please, just Sean."

I made sure he could hear the smile in my voice. I couldn't stop wooing the Ryan brothers until the ink was dry on those contracts. "All right then, Sean, we'll see you tonight."

After I hung up, I did a happy dance in my living room. Marley wanted to be in Ireland. She wanted their soil, their air. She wanted to see what the magic of that country could do to her plants. I pulled up my texts, wanting to let her know the good news.

Avory: The Ryan brothers are signing our contracts! They're bringing them by the office this evening along with some top-shelf whiskey to celebrate.

Crue: Thanks for the invite.

I jerked back, blinking rapidly, trying to understand why Crue texted me back when I'd meant to text my younger sister. Dammit. He was the last person I messaged last night. Fucking technology.

Avory: That was supposed to go to MVP. You're not invited anywhere.

I closed out of that mistake of a text chain and sent one to the correct spawn instead.

Avory: The Ryan brothers are signing our contracts! They're bringing them by the office this evening along with some top-shelf whiskey.

I checked and double-checked that the chain I'd opened was to Marley. Then I thought I'd kill two birds with one stone and add Jett as well.

Marley: Great job you two! I'll see if mom can watch the baby so T and I can celebrate.

Jett: Well, now we know what it takes for Marley to use an exclamation point. Multi billion dollar contracts, Irish soil, and top shelf whiskey.

Avory: And successfully pimping out her family members.

Marley: One Ryan brother is gay, one is straight. I made the right choice sending you two, and we all know it.

Avory: Jett was flirty with both.

Jett: I wasn't flirty, I was charming. Avory rubbed herself on Sean like a cat in heat.

Marley: Sean is the gay one.

Jett: Oh.

Avory: Hahahahahahahahahahaha

Jett: Then yes, it might have seemed like I was flirting.

Marley: Doesn't matter. Contracts are signed and I'm proud of both my little whores.

Avory: Do we have a human resources department?

Marley: Devin. Good luck.

I hadn't been rubbing myself on him like a cat in heat. He was gay, and I was enjoying the male conversation. I loved listening to him talk. Sean was handsome, and his brother was gorgeous. They were funny and charismatic. I'd stayed away from Emmet because he was engaged, and the last thing I wanted anyone to think was that I was making a play for someone who was taken. That would shed a terrible light on me, as well as MJ Botanicals.

Crue: What time are drinks?

Ugh. He was like a bad rash that wouldn't go away.

Avory: You're not invited.

Crue: You're such a child.

Avory: You're such a delusional douche.

Crue: See you tonight, baby.

Chapter Eighteen

Avory

Now

Contracts were filed, the ink was dry, and the whiskey was delicious. Jett, Devin, Marley, Talon, and I were in the lobby of MJ Botanicals. The Ryan brothers brought a case of their finest whiskey, and Devin had appetizers catered in from Austin. It was a small party, but it was a good time.

"So, love, tell me what it's like growing up with rock stars for parents?" Sean sipped from his glass, leaning toward me in a way that didn't put me on edge.

I laughed lightly, the sound honed to perfection over the years: kind and self-deprecating. "It was less interesting than you'd think. How was growing up with whiskey flowing like water?"

"It was fucking fantastic." He winked, his grin taking over his whole handsome face. He had dark brown hair that was styled to absolute perfection. "For the most part at least. I'm sure you can relate though. There's good and bad with being born into a famous family. People always want something from you. Can't trust who your true friends are."

I polished off my first glass, nodding when Sean offered me another two fingers. "Our parents kept us out of the public eye, at all costs." I pointed to the glass doors. "We grew up on that compound across the road. And we were pretty much sequestered there." Although I'd never complained about it. I had my family. I had Cash and Crue. I didn't need anything else. And if I did, I simply snuck out and found it.

"How many of there are you?"

"There were ten of us kids: Landry, Beau, Halen, Evie, Cash, Crue, me, Jett, Marley, and Emmie." His eyes went wide. "But now Landry has three sons, Halen has a daughter and one on the way. Cash's wife is pregnant, Marley has Co, who you met the other day, and Emmie has a baby girl."

"So ten kids, with eight grandbabies and counting? That's a good-size family for four ex-rockers." Sean crossed one leg over the other, the picture of business elegance. "At least you're never lonely, are you?"

I smiled, loving the way *you* sounded more like *yah*. But the truth was, all of us felt lonely at one time or another. We had each other, and we had so much love surrounding us, but that didn't mean we didn't have to go through the trials and tribulations of growing up.

"Crue, hey, man, glad you could make it." Emmet stood from where he'd been chatting with Jett, extending his hand to the ex-love of my life who'd waltzed in like he was the king of the world. Such swagger, always. It was infuriating.

"Wouldn't have missed it." He shook Emmet's hand, and then shot a wink my way.

I glared at him, trying my best to make his blond head explode with the powers of my mind.

"Careful, love, you'll give yourself an aneurism." Sean topped off my drink, distracting me from Crue. "What's the story there? Isn't Crue another one of the Devil's Share offspring?"

I sat back in my seat, crossing my legs and leaning closer to Sean. It was an automatic response to the threat of Crue in my space. I had trained myself to ignore him, to put my attention and focus on someone, anyone, else. "Crue Matthews, son of Luke and Harlow Matthews, heir to a third of the RiffRaff Records fortune. And my first love."

"Ah, that makes sense then." Sean put his hand on my knee, winking at me when I looked up in question. "Every cell in your body hardened to stone when he walked in." He tapped his fingers playfully against my bare leg. "And you turned to me like you were seeking shelter from a storm."

I smiled, loving that Sean was instantly on my side, instantly playing my game. Maybe he'd grown up being a brat like I had. We recognized that in each other. "I was enamored with him, and he broke my heart."

"A tale as old as time."

I sighed, sipping my drink. "I got over it, for the most part. But I recently broke up with my boyfriend, and it seems Crue has decided it's time for us to get back together."

"He's gorgeous." Sean eyed him appreciatively over the rim of his crystal glass.

"He's an entitled asshole who shattered my tiny teenage heart into a million pieces." I rested my chin on my palm. "But he's still the best sex I've ever had." Wow. That was some good whiskey. I hadn't admitted that to anyone, including myself.

"That's a shame, love." Sean turned to me, true pity evident on his face. "If the sex was that good, why not give him another romp? You're single, he's single, and from what you're telling me, he's interested."

Hm. *Give him another romp?* I'd never thought of that. I had spent so much energy getting Crue out of my mind and my heart that the possibility of ever letting him touch me again hadn't even entered my brain. But the other night, his anger had turned me on. Then his texts, and the memories that'd been swamping me. Crue could still get me going, that was for fucking sure. No one made me feel the way Crue could make me feel. No one had ever been able to play my body the way he had.

I let myself look at Crue, really look at him for the first time in what felt like an eternity. He was sexy, he always had been. Blond hair, light eyes, muscles that seemed to only get bigger as the years dragged on.

"He looks like Thor."

I snorted, hiding my smile behind my glass. "He has the hammer to match too."

Sean threw his head back, laughing loudly, his hand still on my leg. Crue's attention immediately flew to the two of us sitting together in the corner. I watched as his eyes moved from my face to Sean's hand on my skin, then back again. He didn't like that. He didn't like someone touching what he thought of as his.

"You're mine, baby, all fucking mine."

"Was I supposed to tell him that?" Another one of his teammates had propositioned me at a party, inviting me to come see his new truck. Insert eye roll.

"He touched you." Crue's fists were clenched at his sides, his anger barely contained.

I climbed into his lap, astride him the way he liked. "But he's gone, and it's you and me here in this dark truck...in this empty field." I tangled my hands in his hair, pulling on it hard like he did to mine. "Make me scream, Crue."

"He's coming this way, love," Sean whispered low, drawing me out of another terrible flashback. I swallowed what was left of my whiskey, needing the distraction and the liquid courage.

"Sean, congratulations. MJ Botanicals is good business." Crue shook Sean's hand, raising his whiskey glass in salute. "Good like this whiskey you and your brother brought."

Crue was talking like he, Sean, and Emmet were old friends, and I found it incredibly annoying. I curled my hand around Sean's arm. "This whiskey *is* delicious." I took another small sip. "I can't wait to tour the distillery when I'm in Ireland."

Marley let us know that we'd all probably be making a few trips once the new location was up and running. Quality control and all that.

Sean, my new best friend, played along. "Mmm, I'm going to enjoy showing you around, love."

I liked when he called me "love." I liked the lilt in his voice and I relished the sour look my enjoyment put on Crue's face. "Maybe I should spend part of the year with you and Emmet. I'm sure you'll need help once the build breaks ground." Not that I knew the first fucking thing about construction.

"You are welcome any time." Sean grabbed my hand off his arm, kissing the back of it. "You say the word, and I'll send the jet."

Crue rolled his eyes. "She has her own jet."

I didn't. RiffRaff and MJ Botanicals shared a jet. But I was intentionally jabbing him. The jealous tone in Crue's voice let me know how well I was doing. "It's always so much more fun to ride someone else's though, isn't it?"

Sean chuckled, kissing the back of my hand again, his lips lingering this time.

Crue's gaze latched on Sean kissing my hand, and then Crue's lips twitched. That didn't bode well for me.

"Avory." Crue crouched down in front of me, completely ignoring Sean. "Let me drive you home."

I didn't need him to drive me anywhere. I could walk to my parents' house from here, or crash at Marley's. Or even Jett's for that matter. There were about a dozen safe places for me to sleep tonight that did not involve Crue's help.

Sean leaned closer, speaking against the shell of my ear, Crue tracking Sean's movements. "If Thor's hammer is that magnificent, why not go another couple rounds? If you're over him, what could it hurt?"

I smiled, which I'm sure only bothered Crue, but that was the point, wasn't it? It looked like Sean and I were sharing some intimate moment, something more than two new friends commiserating. If only Crue knew what I was contemplating.

What could it hurt? Maybe him. But certainly not me. I grinned, handing Sean my empty glass with a wink before letting Crue help me out of my seat.

Game on, fucker.

Chapter Nineteen

Crue

Now

Avory was tipsy, that was the only reason she'd let me lead her by the hand out of the MJ Botanical's lobby. I knew Sean Ryan was gay, and I knew that she'd been trying to make me jealous. More to the point: Avory still cared. She still held a flame for me, her first love. Her only love if I had any say in the matter. She looked beautiful. Her black dress hugged her curves perfectly. Her long toned legs were on display, and leaning into Sean at the sight of me had only hiked her short dress even higher. There wasn't a day that had gone by in the last five years that I didn't crave the feel of her skin against mine.

"I love the way you feel." I moved inside her, my gaze locked on hers. Avory was the most beautiful girl in the world, always. But the way she looked when she came apart in my arms was mesmerizing.

She arched her neck, pushing her naked chest against mine. "Crue."

I couldn't help but smile at the way she moaned my name. It was one word, but it spoke volumes. I could read Avory like a well-worn copy of a favorite book. She wanted more, she wanted me to let go. She was begging me to love her.

Avory rolled her head on the passenger seat, turning to face me. "I could have walked home, you know?"

I cleared the lust from my throat the small memory had created. "I was headed back to the compound anyway." Emmet Ryan had invited me to their mini celebration before Avory had mistakenly texted me. He and I had hit it off while I was coordinating their trip here. Once I knew Avory was going to be in attendance too, I was all in. Which wasn't stalking. I'd pulled that packet out of the trash in Marley's office and read it to be sure.

"Are you going to keep doing this? Keep showing up everywhere I am, texting me in the middle of the night?" She turned to stare out the window as we pulled into the Devil's Share gates. She waved to the guard and I swear I could see him blush in the dim light of his post. Avory had that effect on people, on men in particular. She was so beautiful, so innately sexy, even when she wasn't trying. "Is this your new normal?"

I tightened my hands on the steering wheel, contemplating her questions. Was this my new normal? No. "This is me waking up from five years of bullshit."

"Excuse me?" Avory whirled around, her long hair flying like a silky fan. "Bullshit?"

I passed her parents' house, turning the corner and heading to the old red barn instead. "Yeah, baby, bullshit." I drove the rest of the way to my house before putting my truck in park. "You've been throwing this temper tantrum for half a decade and I'm done being your whipping boy." I'd paid my penance, Marley and Katie were spot on. It was time Avory owned up to the part she played in our demise when we were kids.

"Temper tantrum?" She laughed, but the sound held no humor. "Are you fucking insane? You cheated on me."

I rolled my eyes, which, I was sure, only further pissed her off. "Cheated? Come on. I didn't fuck her. I didn't even touch her. She kissed me. I kissed her back. She took her shirt off and I tossed her off me." When I was in the thick of it, when I could see the hurt and betrayal in Avory's gaze every time I looked at her, I felt like the lowest of the low. But time and age had brought a new clarity to the situation. It was high time I shared that with her.

"I'm sorry I hurt you, but you hurt me too. And my reasons for doing what I did had nothing to do with me, and everything to do with you and my twin. You know that. You've always known that. And I'm done letting you punish me. *Us*. Punish us."

"There is no us, Crue." Her brow furrowed as she took in her surroundings. "Why are we here? I thought you were taking me home."

"And we both fucking know that you agreed to come with me for one reason and one reason only." Once upon a time I'd known

Avory, better than she knew herself. And the look in her eyes back at MJ Botanicals was one I recognized all too well.

I got out of the car, leaving her in there to pout. She could either stay here with me like she'd originally intended or walk back to her childhood home. I opened the front door, using the keypad with a passcode every one of my cousins knew by heart. I flipped on the lamp in the living room, taking off my suit jacket and tossing it on the back of the couch. I couldn't help but smirk when I heard the front door close, and I *felt* Avory step inside.

She was standing in the entryway, her arms crossed over her chest and the toe of her shiny black Louboutin tapping in irritation. She was mad that she couldn't shake me. She wanted to play coy and act like this wasn't exactly what she wanted when she'd climbed inside my truck.

I had other plans.

"Take off your dress."

Her jaw dropped open in outrage and it took everything inside me not to laugh at the absurdity of her expression. "What? You can't be serious."

I removed my tie, tossing it on top of my suit jacket. "Avory, you haven't willingly gotten in a car with me since you were seventeen years old and I can't recall the last time you let me hold your hand." I started to unbutton my shirt. "We both know why you agreed to let me take you home tonight. So take off your fucking dress."

She narrowed her pretty eyes. "Arrogant asshole."

"Self-righteous spoiled brat." I lifted my chin, silently daring her to leave.

She dragged her lower lip through her straight white teeth, her eyes darting to my abs. "This means nothing."

I shrugged. "Whatever you say." She was lying to me, but she was lying to herself as well so I figured I'd give her that one.

She reached behind her, unzipping her sexy black dress before letting it fall off her shoulders and pool around her heels. She was wearing a black strapless bra underneath, panties that matched. I schooled my expression, trying like hell to look unaffected when I was anything but.

This was the first time I'd seen Avory's body bared to me like this in so fucking long I nearly cried. I felt like a man dying of thirst. I wanted to drop to my knees and worship her the way she deserved.

But I was afraid that much emotion would scare her off, would make her leave.

So I lifted my chin, stared down at her like she was nothing more than a toy I thought I'd lost ages ago. "Come here." I pointed to the ground in front of me, clenching my molars together at the ire that flared in her gorgeous eyes. I was pissing her off. But I was also turning her on.

She stepped over her dress, crossing the room to me. "What now, Crue?"

What now, Crue. That's what she'd asked me when we were kids sneaking around by the back gate. I'd made her cancel her plans, and then I'd hauled her body onto my lap and kissed her senseless.

My arm snapped out and wrapped around her slim waist as I dragged her against me. I didn't give either of us time to change our minds, time to think about what would happen when the sun came up. I fused my lips to hers, barely holding in my sigh of relief.

I was home.

After all these years, I was finally where I was supposed to be.

My tongue tangled with hers, both of us fighting for dominance. I'd win, because she wanted me to. I knew what Avory had been missing. I knew what my girl was after. And I knew I was the only one who could ever give it to her.

I picked her up, her long legs encircling my hips. I carried her up the stairs, my hands on her ass and my mouth still playing with hers. I kicked my bedroom door shut and then tossed her onto my bed. Her hair fanned out around her and she bounced against my pillows.

"This means nothing."

I smirked, knowing that arguing with her right now would only delay what we both needed. "Whatever you say, baby." I unbuttoned my pants, sliding them and my boxer briefs down my legs. I watched, satisfied, as her gaze moved up and down my naked body. Her lips parted, a small gasp escaping.

She'd missed me as much as I'd missed her. Her words might deny it, but her body never could.

"Take off the rest, baby."

Her eyes shuttered as she reached behind her back and unclasped her bra, then dangled it over the edge of the bed before dropping it. She slid her hands down her body, teasing herself as she tempted me, stuck her fingers in her panties and lifted her ass to wriggle the lace down her legs. She flicked a foot and sent the panties flying.

I put my palms on her knees, spreading them wide and pinning them down to the mattress. I dipped low, placing kisses on her inner thighs. I wanted to feast on her. I wanted her pliant and—

"No." Her hands tangled in my hair, pulling my head up. "This is sex, Crue. Nothing more."

So she was going to stick with that game? Fine. I didn't need my tongue in her pussy to make her mine again. I nodded toward the edge of the bed. "Grab a condom."

She took a deep breath, like she was steadying herself, before reaching between the mattress and the box spring. She ripped one off the long strip and then flicked it at me, eyebrow raised in defiance. She wouldn't put it on for me, and her expression was daring me to try to make her. But I knew when to pick my battles.

I slid on the condom, the contact to my dick making tingles race up my spine. I was so fucking turned on having her spread before me. If I didn't get my shit together, this would be over a hell of a lot sooner than I wanted it to be. I needed to keep her here. I needed to make this night last until dawn.

I needed her exhausted and sated.

I needed her to let me hold her.

I needed her defenses down.

I moved up her body, planting my hands on either side of her beautiful face, positioning the head of my cock at her entrance. Her breathing was shallow, and I was sweating already. We were both faking it. Both trying to act like what was happening between us meant nothing.

I gripped her slender throat in my hand, pushing into her pussy until I couldn't possibly go any farther. I closed my eyes, trying like hell to slow my pounding heart. Emotion clogged my throat. Tears threatened the back of my eyes.

This meant everything.

Her back arched off the bed, a soft moan escaping. I pulled out, almost all the way, and then surged forward again. I watched her face, the way she bit her bottom lip, the way her eyebrows drew in. I squeezed her throat, knowing that she'd fucking love it. She whimpered, her nails clawing at my bare back. "Open your eyes and tell me what you want, baby."

I wanted to hear her say it. I wanted her to put words to everything she'd been missing for the last five years.

"Harder, Crue." Her gaze collided with mine. "Please, I need...it."

You. I need you. That's what she was going to say. It was working. This was all working. She was lowering that wall, she was remembering the way we loved each other, the way no one else ever could. I hammered into her, giving her exactly what she wanted, moving her body up the mattress with each thrust.

She was moaning, clawing at my flesh while whispering my name on fucking repeat. I moved my hand from her throat to her hair, fisting it, making her arch that pretty neck. I dipped low, nipping at then sucking on her skin. I felt like a man possessed. I wanted her to wear my mark. I wanted her to think of me tomorrow, I wanted her to wake up wanting more.

"You feel so fucking good wrapped around my dick, baby, you know that?" My lips were against her ear, my words spurring her on. "So fucking tight," I growled, the sound foreign to my ears. "No one else fill you up the way I do?" She bit her lips together, refusing to answer me. I tugged her hair harder. "Tell me."

She shook her head, her nails most likely drawing blood on my back.

"Fucking *tell* me." I needed to break her just a little.

She clenched her jaw, defiance in her eyes. So I stopped. I paused mid-thrust, trailing my hand to her sharp jaw, making her look at me. I knew she hated me, but that thin line was dissolving and I couldn't help but push her.

"No." She gripped my ass in her hands, urging me to keep going. "No one has ever been able to fill me the way you do." I kept my victorious smile to myself. "Now stop fucking talking, you're ruining it." She shot up, placing a searing bite over my heart, punishing me and turning me on at the same time.

I pulled all the way out, flipping her over and reentering her again, driving into her over and over. I wrapped her hair in my fist, dragging her body up and against my own. I kissed her neck, panting in her ear. "Good. Now fucking scream my name, baby, just like you used to." I pushed her back down, pounding into her.

Her pussy clenched around my dick, my name on her lips as she milked me fucking dry.

Chapter Twenty

Avory

Now

Crue thought last night was the beginning of us, but really it was nothing more than me scratching an itch. I was curious if things between us would be the way I remembered, the way they'd been when we were teenagers. They hadn't. They were *better*. Crue was always able to blow my fucking mind. But the way he'd made me feel last night? That was something more: it was absolutely decadent. Which pissed me off for obvious reasons. I'd *suspected* that no one would ever be able to make me feel pleasure the way Crue did. Now I was sure.

How was I supposed to date anyone else? How was I supposed to look forward to sex with my next boyfriend when I knew he'd never measure up to my first? I groaned, covering my face with me hands.

"Problem, baby?"

I sighed, peeking through my fingers at a still-naked Crue. He'd never had any shame, any modesty. And it looked like that hadn't changed either. He was standing at the foot of the bed, a cup of steaming coffee in his hand. "Is that coffee for me?" I sounded hopeful because I was. I needed coffee. I had a slight emotional hang over.

"No." He got back in bed, handing me the white porcelain mug. "But you can have some."

It seemed intimate, sharing coffee in bed. But I certainly didn't want him to watch me stumble around and try to find my clothes so I could go make my own. "Thank you." I may dislike the sex god, but I still had manners.

I sipped it, wincing when it burned my tongue. I needed to get out of there. I shouldn't've stayed the night. It would have been more on brand for me to walk out the door as soon as I came down from my orgasmic high. I was trying to help him move on. I was trying to prove that he didn't matter and he never would. Sleeping cuddled up next to him was misleading for both of us.

He'd fucked me senseless, which I was sure was his plan all along. Made me come so hard I was limp and pliant. He'd basically molded me into a ball after that, spooning me as I drifted off to sleep. Asshole.

"I've got to go." I took one more sip of coffee, then slipped out of bed, wrapping his crisp white sheet around my body. "I have, um, stuff." I cringed at my awkwardness. *Stuff?* For fuck's sake. I didn't have cool plans. I needed to work, like I was sure he did.

"Okay." He sat back against his headboard, the one that I was surprised hadn't put a damn hole in the wall last night.

I whipped the sheet around me as leaned down to pick up my bra, undies, and shoes. I turned to the door. "Have a good day."

"Have a good day" was about as great as "stuff." I needed to get the fuck out of Crue's house before his smug ass thought I was fumbling my words because he flustered me.

I left his room without another word, gathered my dress in the living room, and put on my clothes. I stepped into my heels, then strode confidently to the front door.

I knew I looked good, even first thing in the morning. My hair was no doubt messy in that overly sexed way. And my eyeliner from last night probably had me rocking a smoky eye. But after I opened the front door, I realized, hot or not, I would be doing the walk of shame in front of any and all family members who happened to see me. I was still wearing last night's outfit. I was in five-inch heels. I took a deep breath, trying to calmly think of a solution to—

"Problem, baby?"

I turned, glancing over my shoulder to find Crue leaning against the stair railing with his muscular arms crossed over his even more muscular chest. *Problem, baby?* Was that all he could fucking say this morning? This whole fiasco was one giant damn problem. I was loath to admit my current dilemma, but didn't see that I had a choice. "If I walk out of here looking like this, and someone sees me…"

"They'll know I fucked you until you went hoarse from screaming my name?" His smirk made me want to fly across the room and punch him in the face.

I shifted on my feet, weighing my options. If one of our cousins saw us, I could simply chalk it up to a night of bad decision-making. If one of our parents saw us, that would make things a hell of a lot more complicated. Then again, I could always lie and tell them that I'd had too much to drink last night and Crue was nice enough to give me a lift home. "*Problem* solved, asshole." I took off my heels, preparing to hoof it home. "If our parents see me, I'll tell them I over-enjoyed the Irish whiskey, and you were nice enough to drive me home."

"So you'll lie to their faces." Crue nodded. "Seems like the adult thing to do."

"It's one tiny fib." I rolled my eyes, not enjoying his sudden and new high horse. He did drive me home. I'd leave out the part where we got naked once we got here.

Crue pulled his shirt from where it was dangling in the back pocket of his ripped blue jeans. "I'll take you back to your parents' house."

So the drive of shame, then. I sighed as I followed Crue out of the barn. Why did this seem like such a great idea last night? Stupid Irish whiskey.

The drive to my parents' house was short and silent. I didn't know what to say to him, and last night's activities kept playing on a loop in my mind. The way he'd tossed me onto the bed, the way he'd pulled my hair, the way he'd growled against my ear, spilling so fucking deep inside me.

I licked my lips, counting down the seconds until I could be out of his truck and away from his intoxicating scent. Should I say thank you for the orgasms? Should I remind him that I hate him and last night meant nothing? No. I needed to keep my mouth shut. I might accidentally ask him to bend me over in the back seat.

When he put the truck in park and turned to me, his wrist resting casually over the steering wheel, I bolted. Like straight up, opened the door and jumped out of the truck. I may have run all the way to my parents' front door.

Texts the next day

Crue: You sore? I'm sure it's been a while since you were rode that hard.

Avory: Says who?

Crue: You, last night. Is every word out of your mouth these days a lie?

Avory: Please stop texting me.

Crue: Sean flew back to Ireland. You miss him? You two seemed close.

Avory: He's great. So kind and handsome. I've already planned a trip to go visit.

Crue: You think he'll introduce you to his boyfriend?

Crue: You still there? Are you thinking back on how you flirted with a gay man to make me jealous? I agree. It was pretty pathetic.

Avory: Fuck off Crue. I wasn't trying to make you jealous.

Crue: Lie.

Avory: You weren't supposed to be there. You walked in and it shocked me.

Crue: Holy fucking shit. Did you just tell the truth?

Avory: I hate you.

Crue: Lie.

Texts the day after that

Crue: Jett's birthday is this weekend.

Avory: I've known him since he was born. I'm well aware of when Jett's birthday is.

Crue: He wants to party down by the tank. Cheap beer, bonfire, like the old days.

Avory: MVP texted me already.

Crue: Does that mean you're coming?

Avory: Yes.

Crue: Cool. You want to leave your car at my house and then we can walk down together?

Avory: Why in the holy hell would I do that?

Crue: Uh, to save you from another walk of shame conundrum, obviously.

Avory: Hahahahahahahahahahahahahahhahahaha you are so fucking out of your mind if you think I'm staying the night with you. Ever. Again.

Crue: We'll see, baby spawn.

And texts the day after that

Crue: What are you wearing?

Avory: An irritated frown. Stop texting me.

Crue: What time are you coming over tonight?

Avory: Are you high?

Crue: It's Jett's birthday party, remember?

Avory: Of course I fucking remember.

Crue: I thought you were leaving your car here.

Avory: Seriously. Are you actually high or did you fall and hit your head? I am not leaving my car at your house. I am not staying with you tonight.

Crue: Here's what's going to happen. You're going to drive your fucking ass to the red barn, then you and I are going to walk to Jett's birthday party together. We're going to laugh with our family and we're going to get buzzed on cheap beer. Then, I'm going to lay you out on the kitchen island and eat you for a midnight snack.

Crue: I'll take your lack of response as a Yes Sir.

Crue: See you tonight, baby.

Chapter Twenty-One

Crue

Now

I'd like to be all smug male and tell you that fucking Avory had been the highlight of the other night. But I'd be lying. And unlike Avory, I was trying to lean more toward truths these days. Holding her in my arms while she slept, waking up to find her next to me. Those had been the best parts of being with her again. Don't get me wrong, the sex was hot as hell, better than I even remembered. But touching her, kissing her, seeing her complete surrender. Those were the things I'd missed the most.

I couldn't tell her that though, not yet. Instead I had to be an asshole, demanding her compliance. I didn't like that she was holding back, that she was trying to keep a good amount of distance between us even after the other night. I wanted the games to be over, but she was obviously still playing.

It'd been three days since I'd seen her, and I missed my girl.

I hadn't seen my girl in days, in five days to be exact. Cheer camp overlapped baseball camp. First-world high-schoolers' problems. I'd texted her the instant Cash and I pulled back on the compound, letting her know I'd be climbing through her window in a matter of minutes. I needed her legs wrapped around me, I needed to hear her whisper my name as she fell apart in my arms.

I was horny and I missed my girlfriend. A lethal combination and it had me not giving a shit if someone saw us.

She must have been feeling the exact same though, because the second I hopped out of Cash's Jeep I saw her flying across the field separating our houses. Her dark hair was in a high ponytail, her shorts were miniscule, and her neon yellow sports bra was like lightning in the dark sky.

"I'll tell Mom and Dad Benson forgot his cell in the Jeep and you're taking it to him." Cash patted me on the shoulder, chuckling as he headed up our front steps.

I closed the gap between Avory and me in a few long strides, picking her up as she launched herself into my arms. "You're home."

I smiled, cupping her face in my palms, kissing her lips hungrily as she kept her legs wrapped tight around my waist. "I'm home." I spun us around, propping her tiny body against the side of Cash's still-warm Jeep. I sucked on her shoulder, my hands moving to squeeze her tight little ass. "Fuck, I missed you."

She fumbled behind her, opening the back passenger side door. I lifted her inside, shoving our gear to the floorboards. I had her laid out underneath me and nothing short of a fucking tornado would have been able to stop me from slipping inside her. I pulled off her shorts as she pushed down my jeans, neither one of us caring about anything other than joining our bodies.

She moaned my name as I thrust inside her, bare, damning the consequences. "Fuck, baby, you feel so good."

"Tell me it's not always like this. Tell me that we're different. Tell me we're everything and that's what makes it feels so fucking good."

I wrapped my hand around the base of her slender throat, squeezing until she met my eyes in the dim light from the porch. "It's us, baby." I hammered into her, bruising her neck and her thighs with my punishing grip. "I swear, it's us."

The knock at my front door jolted me out of the steamy memory. No one knocked. Everyone simply entered the code into the keypad and came in uninvited and unannounced. It had to be Avory. She was subtly trying to show me that we weren't close, no matter how many times I made her come the other night.

I opened the door wide, stepping out of her way. She looked edible, making me recall my plan to eat her for my midnight snack. Her jeans were tight, and her shirt only covered half of her torso. Her long dark hair hung board straight, tickling the exposed skin on her back.

I knew she'd meet me at my house. I knew what my demanding text would do to her. And I also knew that once wouldn't be enough. She'd justify it. She already let herself fall into bed with me. She might as well enjoy it while she could. It didn't matter to me, the reason she was here. I was simply pumped that she was.

I grabbed the ice chest I packed for us. I was an adult. I refused to drink cheap beer no matter whose birthday it was. "You ready?"

She nodded, setting her purse on the coffee table. That simple gesture made me have to fight a smile. She was staying, leaving her purse here, her car keys.

"Let's go." I held my hand out, figuring I might as well go for broke.

She shook her head. "No."

No? Then why the hell was she here? I was going to win. Didn't she see that? "Avory, for fuck's—"

"No, Crue." She shook her head, looking down at her feet, alerting me to the fact that she was feeling nervous. "You were right. It would have been stupid of me to act like I'm not going to end up back here at the end of the night. But I'm not walking down to that party like we're still a couple. I'm not." She lifted her chin, becoming the confident Avory once again. "So you go, I'll meet you there."

I wanted to demand she put her hand in mine. But it was her soft tone, the almost defeated note in her voice that made me take a pause. Letting our family see us together, it meant something. They'd all shared in our love, as well as our demise. She was back in my bed. She was back in my life. But she wasn't ready to be back at my side.

And in this, and this alone, I wouldn't push.

Chapter Twenty-Two

Avory

Now

I waited inside the red barn that Crue now called home. I didn't want our family to think we were getting back together, because we sure as fuck were not. And that's exactly what they would assume if we walked down to that party like old friends.

I wanted him to touch me. I wanted him to make me come. But I didn't want him to love me.

I trailed my fingers along the banister, making my way up the stairs that led to the two bedrooms. One had been Jett's, and Crue now used the one that had been Marley's. After they'd moved out, Jett and Marley had offered the place to me. But I'd turned it down. I knew Crue would move back to Texas once Cash and Katie did, and I didn't want to be living on the compound when he returned. I didn't want to see him every day. I didn't want to be that close to him. I'd told myself that it would be easier for *him* that way, but I was starting to suspect I'd done it out of self-preservation.

I stepped into his room, allowing myself one brief moment to close my eyes and fill my lungs with his scent. He smelled the same as he had when we were teenagers. The same cologne, the same soap. When I was in here the other night, I'd refused to spend too much time looking around. I didn't want to seem interested, I didn't want him to think anything about him or his life here mattered.

But I was alone now, and I couldn't seem to decide where to look first. His bed I'd become reacquainted with already, the crisp white sheets and the soft black blankets. His charcoal-colored nightstands held matching thin gold lamps. The whole room had a chic, modern vibe and I wondered who had helped him pick everything out.

There was a collection of framed prints along one wall. Images of him and his brothers, him and Brody at the beach with surfboards in their hands, his baseball team dog piling on top of him after a game-winning home run. I sucked in a sharp breath when my gaze roamed to the next picture.

It was us.

We'd been out on the practice field with Cash. Beau had been there with his camera. It was after he'd returned to the compound to get Halen back. Crue had tossed me over his shoulder, and Beau captured the moment as Crue had smacked my ass and made me giggle.

We looked so fucking carefree.

"Let's skip lunch and go home, we can sneak down to the pool house."

Crue placed me on my feet, palming my ass and pulling me tight against his body.

"You want to go skinny-dipping?"

He threw his head back, chuckling. "Skinny-dip? It's the middle of the day, and all the parents are home." He shook his head. "Even I'm not that fucking bold."

"That's a shame." I stuck out my bottom lip, pouting.

He pushed me up against the cinderblock wall, dipping down to capture my lips. I moaned against his mouth, hiking my thigh up higher on his hip. I wanted more. I didn't care who was watching.

He pulled back, smirking that sexy grin of his. "As soon as the sun goes down."

"You'll take me skinny dipping?" I waggled my eyebrows.

"What my baby wants, my baby gets."

I wrapped my arms around his neck, playing with the hair tickling his neck. "I want you."

"And I want you." He kissed me again. "Only you, forever."

There were so many versions of Crue, and I loved every single one of them. I liked Crue the brother joking with his siblings and playing catch in the empty field beside his house. Crue the asshole glaring at people who dared to talk to us, demanding his way no matter the consequences. But the Crue who loved me, that was my favorite Crue. He made me feel special without letting me act spoiled. He gave me pleasure while riding that dark edge of pain. He was sweet, in the rough way I craved.

"Forever? You promise?" I couldn't help but glance at Halen and Beau. I was sure Beau had promised my big sister they'd be together for the rest of time too. And look what a fucking disaster that had become.

Crue took my chin in his fingers, tilting my face back to him. "We're not them, baby spawn." He kissed me once again, sliding his tongue along my lower lip. "I'll never hurt you."

"You don't know that." I wasn't trying to cause a fight, but I needed his words. I needed him to reassure me. "We could end up hurting each other, whether we mean to or not."

"Then I'd spend the rest of my life kissing the hurt away."

I wiped at the tear rolling down my cheek. It was over five years later and that's exactly what it seemed he was doing. Trying to kiss the hurt away.

Chapter Twenty-Three

Crue

Now

Avory was sitting next me, the fire burning bright in front of us. I wanted to put my arm around her. I wanted to rest my palm on her hip and have her sink against me. But what I wanted and what I was going to get were still two very different things. She'd come down to the tank a couple hours ago, instantly going to her sisters. She ignored me, the way she'd been doing at family gatherings since we broke up by the back gate all those years ago. I watched her from a distance, drinking in the way she laughed, the range of emotions that played across her face while someone told her a story.

She was so beautiful, and so close to being mine again I could almost taste it.

When Avory had gone to sit by the firepit, I'd followed her. I was done observing her at a distance. I wanted to talk to her. I wanted to be next to her. She didn't immediately get up, so I took that as a good sign. "Did you start with my browser history? Or did you snoop through my closet first?" I was teasing, but I also knew the second I left her alone in my house her curiosity would get the best of her.

She glanced at me, smiling against the bottle of beer in her hand. "Your bedroom."

I tskd. "You've already been in there. I'd have started with the closets."

"There's a picture of us up on your wall, the one Beau took when we were in high school."

Beau had framed it for me as a housewarming gift after I moved into the red barn. At first I'd been pissed. But over time, I understood why he'd done it. Avory was a memory worth honoring. "It was a gift." That was the only explanation I could give her right now, while we were down here surrounded by our cousins. "You ready to go?" I waited until she turned to look at me, and then I winked.

Avory shook her head. "Stop winking at me." Then flipped her hair over her shoulder, extremely reminiscent of the sixteen-year-old version of herself. "It's annoying."

"You used to think it was hot." She used to think it was hot because she knew the secrets behind it. She knew what I was promising.

"I used to think a lot of things were hot." She was being a brat, and bringing up that picture and my room had me feeling vulnerable. I couldn't let her see me be so soft. I needed to remind her who was in charge, who was running this new shit show. I wanted her back, and I was convinced this was the way I had to do it.

My hand shot out, wrapping around the base of her throat before she could protest. "I remember, baby." I watched with satisfaction as her eyes danced with fire. She fucking loved being touched like this. I wondered how long it'd been since someone had nailed her the way she liked it, the way I had the other night: rough and wild, taking and never asking for permission.

She dug her sharp nails into the flesh of my wrist, demanding I let her go. "I'm not yours to touch like this anymore, Crue."

I leaned close, pissing her off further as I put my lips against the shell of her ear. "You'll always be mine, Avory."

"Tell me I'll always be yours."

"You'll always be mine, baby." I let my hands trail up her ribcage, loving how big my palms looked as they spanned across her body. "Always."

There would never be anyone else I'd ever want like this. I craved her. I was addicted to every single inch of my girl.

"You're playing with fire." Brody came to sit next to me after Avory got up and left in what could only be described as a huff. "She looks pissed enough to explode."

He handed me a fresh beer and I instantly popped the top. "Good. Reaction is what gets her back in my bed." Reaction and a bit of Irish whiskey apparently.

"Is that what you're after? You want to fuck your first love?"

I wouldn't tell him that I already had, a few times, and that I planned on doing it again in a matter of minutes. "Yes, and no." I sighed, knowing that Avory and I wouldn't make a lot of sense to him. "Avory is tougher than she looks, tougher than she lets people see. I need to get her defenses down, I need to remind her how good we were together. And then, maybe, she'll let me back in."

"So you need to get into her pants in order to get into her heart?"

"Yep." I needed her to be weak with me, and the only way she'd let me hold her, let me love her, was after she let me fuck her. If I walked up to her right now and tried to take her hand, she'd probably punch me in the balls.

"I feel ya."

I raised my eyebrows. "Really?"

He nodded, lips pursed. "I'm pretty sure Landry fell in love with my dick before she did any other part of me."

"Word." Landry lifted her beer above her head, making us laugh and letting us know she was eavesdropping in on our conversation.

I drained the bottle in my hand, tossing the empty into the ice chest I brought with me. I'd come get it tomorrow. I'd leave the rest of the brews in there for my cousins. I got to my feet, dusting off my jeans and making a beeline for Avory.

She was standing with Jett and Devin, laughing at something that cocky-ass fucker had said. I took her elbow in my hand, gently pulling her away from them and into the shadows. I was done being a bystander in her life tonight. I wanted to be the star. "It's time to go." She looked up at me, defiance in her eyes. "Go back to the house, baby, or I'll throw you over my shoulder in front of everyone and take you there myself."

She rolled her eyes, gritting out a short, "Fine. Asshole."

When she started telling people bye, I couldn't hide my satisfied smirk. She'd go to my house, and I'd wait five minutes and leave too. My girl would be back in my bed, back in my arms. I'd get to hold her. I'd get to feel her heartbeat against my own. Fuck. I wish she'd just give in. I wished she'd let me love her again.

"Could you stare any harder?" My twin came up, cocking his head to the side and following my line of sight. "I'm assuming she's not leaving the compound tonight?"

I snorted. "You'd assume correctly." That girl wasn't going anywhere until the sun came up. She'd be lucky if I let her leave then either. I was feeling slightly unhinged and incredibly in love-lust.

Cash took a sip of his beer. "So, what's going on with you two?"

"What's going on with you two?"

"What are you talking about?" Sweat instantly pooled in my armpits.

"I saw you. You were climbing out of Avory's window last night." I felt like a deer caught in the headlights. Our secret was out. *"I know what I saw. I was leaving Halen's room, Crue. So stop lying to me."*

I didn't set out to keep anything from my brother, but somewhere along the way, I had. I didn't feel guilty about it, not really. Cash had his own shit to deal with. Hell, he was still handling the fallout from Beau leaving Halen after her miscarriage. And that was some heavy crap right there. But I guessed now was as good a time as any to come clean with my best friend.

"We're, uh, hooking up." Ugh. That sounded so fucking lame.

"You're hooking up? With Avory? You're fucking Avory? Are you fucking kidding me?" Cash fisted his hands in front of my face, like he was thinking about punching me. *"Since when, and what the hell are you thinking?"*

"First of all, lower your goddamn voice, before I lower it for you." I stepped forward, grabbing his arm and dragging him away from my bedroom door. *"Second of all, no, I'm not fucking her. Or at least, I haven't, yet."*

"Did you learn nothing from what happened with Hales and Beau?" I wondered if my cousins knew they'd become a cautionary tale.

"We aren't Halen and Beau. We aren't. I wouldn't leave her. I would never hurt her like that." If anything, being with Avory these last few weeks made me hate my older cousin, made me hate what he'd done to Halen. *"I care about her, man, like, I really fucking care."*

"Are you guys dating? Is that what you're telling me? You're with Avory, and no one else?" Cash sounded skeptical, but I couldn't blame him. I got around.

"There's no one else, I don't want anyone else." The thought of being with another girl made me sick to my stomach. Sometimes, late at night when Avory was lying in my arms, I wished I could go back

and save every part of me for her. The way she'd saved herself for me.

"How did this even happen?"

That was the million-dollar question, wasn't it? "I don't know, honestly. It was like one day I woke up and she looked different to me. I saw her standing outside her house waiting for us to pick her up and she...she took my breath away. It was as if overnight, everything changed." I sounded like a sap, but that was the truth as I remembered it. "I started getting jealous when guys would ask her out. I broke some sophomore's nose when I saw him bring her home past curfew."

"How long has this been going on?"

"Few weeks." I collapsed back down onto my bed, picking up the gaming controller I'd been playing with before Cash had barged in. "I was down by the back gate one night and I caught her trying to sneak off the compound. I made her cancel her plans, and then we sort of jumped each other."

"Anyone else know?"

"No." I handed him the second controller when he sat down beside me. "I was going to tell you, soon, I swear. It's new and it's...a lot. You've already got Halen's shit to deal with and we didn't want you to have to lie for us too."

"I'm your twin, Crue. I'm with you guys all the way." He held his fist out so I could bump it. "'Til the end, bro."

"'Til the end."

"Hey. You going to answer me or keep staring off in the distance like a nutcase?" Cash bumped his shoulder into mine, bringing me back to the here and now.

"Sorry." I sighed. "I guess you could say I've made some progress." Slight progress and motherf'in baby steps. That was exactly what was going on between Avory and me at the moment.

"You banged her, but she's still trying to act like you're the dirt on her shoes?"

I nodded, lips pursed. "Yep." Cash knew me, and he knew Avory. It wasn't hard for him to hit the nail on the head with his summarization.

Cash put his hand on my shoulder, shaking me gently. "We're here for you, bro, 'til the end."

I turned to him, smiling at the words that had been in my memories moments ago. He'd been by my side, no matter what, since day one. It didn't matter if I was going to get us both in trouble, or if I was asking too much of him. He never wavered. "You're a really fucking good brother, you know that?"

"I do, in fact, know that."

Cash had been stepping up for me my whole life. He'd helped me keep my secrets, he'd sacrificed himself at the altar of my and Avory's love. "We didn't deserve your help, Avory and me." I wasn't sure when I'd come to that conclusion, or when I'd decided to go there with him tonight. But the words felt right, cathartic. I should have said them years ago. He stared at me, like he wasn't sure how to respond. "We were selfish, and self-serving. And I'm so fucking sorry."

Cash swallowed, nodding his head. "I appreciate that." He cleared this throat, emotion heavy in the air between us. "Now, go work on getting your girl back."

I smiled as I walked away. Every one of our cousins still called Avory my girl, and I wasn't sure they'd ever stopped.

Chapter Twenty-Four

Avory

Now

I was sitting in Crue's living room, staring at the black screen of his TV. I'd been arguing with myself since I'd walked in here a few minutes ago. Should I leave? Prove to him that he wasn't the boss of me, that he wasn't in control the way he thought he was? Should I stay? Have a good time, and let him make me feel good for a few hours? I was weighing the pros and cons of each option when the front door opened and Crue filled the entryway. His presence took up a space and my body noticed even when I refused to let my heart weigh in.

His white shirt was threadbare, on purpose I was sure. His jeans were worn and tattered, his boots untied. He looked messy, but in a way that worked for him. He cleaned up for work, wearing expensive suits and shiny shoes. But I preferred this Crue. The relaxed badass.

"Took you long enough." I studied my nails, going for nonchalant when really my mind was racing. "I almost left."

He shut the door, throwing the deadbolt into place. "And yet, you're still here." He grabbed his shirt from the back, pulling it off and tossing it onto the couch beside me.

He was right. I was still there. I was still on my family's compound. I was still waiting with bated breath for Crue Matthews's next move. I wasn't too sure how that made me feel. Was I stuck, stagnant in this life of mine? Or was I exactly where I was always supposed to be? "I'm not staying the night this time, Crue. One and done." I couldn't answer any of my own questions, and until I could, I needed to draw some clear lines between the two of us.

"One?" He chuckled, unbuckling his jeans as he made his way across the room, coming closer with every step. I felt like I was being stalked like prey. "We'll see, baby spawn."

He picked me up, my legs wrapping around him automatically. He carried me effortlessly into the kitchen, holding me with one arm and clearing everything off the center island with the other. A bowl full of fruit went crashing to the ground, papers scattering. My heart was racing, my core already clenching. That right there, the recklessness, that was what I'd been missing. That insatiable need. That passion only Crue Matthews could give me.

A few nights ago I'd told him no foreplay, but as he yanked my jeans off my legs, I was already going against my own rules. He ripped my panties, letting them fall to the floor with the ruined apples. He put his palms on my bare thighs, spreading me out before him. His jaw was clenched, his eyes hungry. I couldn't help but watch him enjoy the sight of me. I had butterflies in my stomach. I was shaking on the kitchen counter. I wanted him to touch me and at the same time I wanted him to turn around and walk away, saving us both.

Crue's mouth covered my core, his tongue working my clit as warmth filled my entire body. My hands tangled in his hair, my spine arching. A small gasp left my mouth, and with it, all thoughts of self-preservation.

***

Crue and I were sitting on the kitchen island, side by side, our legs swinging. Since he'd ruined my panties, he let me sit on his t-shirt. After he'd finished feasting on me, like he'd promised he would, he picked a banana up off the floor and we were sharing it.

"I should go." I swallowed the last bite, the one he'd offered to me moments ago. "It's late." I checked my watch, seeing that it was half past midnight. Huh. He'd called me a midnight snack on that text, and he'd stood by it.

He placed his hand on my thigh, his fingers tapping out a static beat. "You're not leaving, baby." His tone was soft, like he almost felt sorry for me. What was he going to do, tie me to his bed and never let me out of this house again? Eventually someone would come looking for me. Our cousins weren't stupid. They knew I was here. My car was parked out front.

"You don't control me." I lifted my chin, turning so I could see his face out of the corner of my eye. "If I want to leave, I'll fucking leave."

He hopped down off the counter, standing in front of me with his muscular pecs on display. Damn he looked good. "But you don't want to leave."

He said it like a statement, and that pissed me off. But he wasn't wrong. I didn't want to leave, not yet anyway. I was already here. I'd already let him back inside my body. I might as well fucking enjoy it. Besides, it didn't mean anything.

Crue palmed my ass, lifting me into his arms. He carried me up the stairs, like he had a few nights ago. I kissed his lips, sucking roughly on his bottom one. He groaned and I smirked. Once his bedroom door was shut, he fell backward onto the large bed, landing with me on top of him. He smacked my ass. "Ride me, baby."

I pursed my lips, my hands on my hips as I stared down at him. He put his palms behind his head, one eyebrow cocked. I could feel him nestled against my thigh, hard as stone. "That's it? 'Ride me, baby'?" I shrugged. "Underwhelmed."

"Underwhelmed?" He chuckled. "I'm pretty sure you were speaking in tongues on that kitchen counter."

He wasn't wrong. He'd fucking blew my mind into a million pieces. I was pretty sure I'd stopped breathing for a solid minute. But I wasn't here to stroke his ego. "I'm not going to hop on your dick because you demand it."

"You said no foreplay, just sex."

"And clearly, we already shot that to shit." I jerked my thumb behind me, indicating what he'd done to me twenty minutes ago.

"Okay." He sat up his lips dangerously close to mine. "But you asked for it."

He tangled his hand in my hair, fusing his mouth to mine. He kissed me deeply, invading every single fucking sense I had. He tugged at my hair as his other arm snaked around my waist, holding me tight against his hard body. I fumbled with his jeans, unbuttoning them, freeing his impressive length. I couldn't think past his kisses, past the feel of him holding me so fucking close. His lips moved to my neck, sucking and kissing his way to my shoulder. He clamped down with his teeth, making me whimper in pleasure. He lifted me with ease.

"Ride me, baby."

He positioned the head of his cock at my entrance and I wasted no time, sinking down on him as his name left my mouth like a damn prayer. His forehead rested against mine, our breath mingling, both of us panting. His hands were in my hair, my nails digging into his back. There was a tiny voice in the back of my mind, screaming at me to stop. But fuck her. Crue was as deep inside me as I could get him, and he was holding me. He was kissing me. He was worshipping me. And mistake or not, I didn't want him to ever fucking quit.

"Baby, fuck, you feel so damn good wrapped around my dick like this." His lips were leaving a burning trail, from my mouth to my shoulder and back again.

My head was back, my breathing ragged. I was so close to the edge, but I didn't want this to be over. "Crue." He flipped us around, slamming into me, the headboard hitting the wall behind it. "Yes, fuck, don't stop." He could read my mind when we were connected like this: he'd always been able to. He knew exactly what I needed, and when I needed it. Every nerve in my body was firing at the same time, so much pleasure that I wanted to fucking cry.

"Come for me, baby." He nipped at the sensitive spot between my shoulder and neck. "Let me hear you scream." He drove inside me, as deep as he could possibly go, grinding his pelvis against my clit. And I did exactly what he demanded. I screamed his fucking name as I shattered around him.

He growled as his fingers tightened in my hair, his lips finding my mine as he spilled inside me.

Chapter Twenty-Five

Avory

Now

I snuck out of Crue's house before the sun came up; that was how I justified what had happened between us—again—to myself. I didn't stay the night. I didn't wake up with him smiling down at me. I got what I came for, twice, and then I left. Sort of.

Currently, I was wrapped in a blanket I'd found on the back of his couch, walking the caliche roads of the compound. The sky was turning a lighter shade of purple, letting the world know that a new day was on its way. After we'd both come down from our high, he'd pulled me to his chest, his fingers dragging up and down my back, and we fell asleep.

I took a deep breath, loving the silence that surrounded me, wiping at the tears that were falling from my eyes. I didn't know what I was doing. I didn't know why I'd fallen back into bed with Crue. I didn't know why I couldn't love Colin the way he loved me. I didn't know why I couldn't leave this place, these people. I was confused, and I was frustrated. And I guess those two things together mixed with the sunrise were making me a little emotional.

When I broke up with Crue, I'd told him I wouldn't cry over him, that I would smile and move the fuck on. And I had. I hadn't fallen apart. I hadn't used one of our cousins as a security blanket. No. I cheered the loudest at all the football games. I was the life of every party I'd attended. I went to college. I dated my ass off. And all the while, I never let the memory of my first love affect me.

I'd buried Crue and all the hurt that accompanied the memory of him down deep, in a locked box that I never even let myself think about opening. But that locked box it seemed had worn through over time. Memories kept escaping, and emotions long since forgotten kept finding their way to the surface.

My cell vibrated in my pocket, the alert making me jump. I knew who it was, and part of me wanted to leave it unread. But that part of me was the same bitch I silenced last night as Crue was fucking me bare.

Crue: Get your ass back in this bed.

I swallowed thickly, wiping away more tears. I couldn't do that. I couldn't go climb into that warm bed with the boy who broke my heart. It was all becoming too familiar, too comfortable. Crue had cheated on me. He'd hurt me. He'd ruined us and I didn't trust him anymore. Right? Right. I needed to remember that. I couldn't let myself fall for him, fall for whatever it was he was trying to pull.

Avory: Can't. Plans.

Crue: Your car is still here.

Avory: Plans are on the compound, stalker. Leave me alone.

Crue: No.

I shoved my cell back into the pocket of my jeans and when the road forked, I took a left. I didn't actually have plans, but I did have plenty of family that lived within walking distance. I waved to the guard at the gate, crossing the empty road and jumping the gate to MJ Botanicals' land. They had a guard too. He recognized me and tipped his hat.

By the time I made it to my sister's house, the sun was rising over the horizon. Her kitchen light was on, so I knew they were up. Co didn't sleep in, ever. She and Talon complained about it all the time. They were perpetually exhausted. I keyed in the code to her door, stepping through. "Hello? No one's naked, right?"

"Well, one of us is." Talon came around the corner, chasing a naked crawling baby. He laughed, scooping him up, making Co giggle. "Here, get your nephew dressed." Talon handed me the kid and the clothes. "It's early, is everything okay?"

I stepped into the living room, sitting on the floor with Co. "I needed to take a walk."

"From Austin?" Talon's eyebrows rose to his blond hairline.

"She stayed at the red barn last night." Marley came in, her dark hair piled on her head and a steaming mug of coffee in her hands.

Talon winced, collapsing on their sectional. "You hooking up with Motley Crue?"

Hooking up. Well. I supposed that was one of the nicer ways to word it. I fished Co's hands out of his sleeves, pulling them through before letting him hold onto my fingers so he could stand up. "Yes."

"How many times now?" Marley smiled when her son dropped back to the ground to crawl over to her. She reached down, picking him up, and got him settled into her lap.

"Twice." I wrinkled my nose. "Like, two nights." I'd come more than twice, thanks to that amazing kitchen counter round.

"And you came here so I could tell you you're making a huge mistake?" Marley questioned, adjusting her glasses.

"I came here because I snuck out of Crue's bed this morning and I needed a reason not to go back yet." I crawled over to the couch and tickled the bottom of Co's feet. "And I wanted to see my favorite nephew."

Marley glanced down at her son, her grin playful. "Don't let her spout that bull to you, kid, you're her only actual nephew." She sighed, passing me her coffee cup. "You want to talk about it? Talk about Crue?"

Talon got to his feet, gathering their son and hoisting him high in the air before cuddling the baby to his chest. "You two chat, Co and I are going to go have breakfast with Brody and his boys." Talon dipped down and kissed the top of my head, then straightened and kissed Marley on the mouth before leaving.

Once I heard the front door closed, I sort of folded. "I don't know what I'm doing."

"Do you normally, though?" Marley took her coffee back, patting the couch next to her.

"I meant with Crue. I don't know what I'm doing with Crue." Leave it to Marley to make you question more than you wanted to. I'd like to think that normally, I had my shit in order. I mean, I was adulting as best I could. I did laundry and cooked for myself. The other day I'd even reorganized my junk drawer.

"Why did you start sleeping with him again if it's so confusing for you?"

"I didn't set out trying to confuse myself." I stole her coffee, taking another sip. "The other night, Sean Ryan and I were talking. I told him that Crue was the best sex I'd ever had. He said, well then why not give it another go. So, I did."

Marley scoffed. "Sean, a man you've only spoken to a handful of times, is the reason you slept with Crue after five years of avoiding him?" She rolled her eyes. "Avory. Your problem is you like to blame other people for the things that happen in your life."

"I'm not blaming him." It wasn't Sean's fault that I slept with Crue, although he was the one who put the idea in my head. "I'm trying to tell you what happened."

"You slept with Crue because you broke up with your boyfriend and your first love has been all up in your head space ever since." She got to her feet, heading to the kitchen, knowing I'd follow. She did that a lot, to all of us. "Now. Why did you sleep with him *again* last night?" She put two bagels in the toaster.

"I don't know. He kept texting me. He knows how to push my buttons and—"

"There you go again." She rested her back against the counter, waiting on her breakfast and handing me my ass. "*He texted me, he pushes my buttons*. No. You're an adult, Avory. *You* are the only person in charge of you. Now. Why did you sleep with him again?"

"I don't know." I threw my hands in the air when her eyes narrowed scarily. "Because I wanted to. Because it felt good. Because I like the way he bosses me around. Because I've been craving that passion. Because I missed it. Because I fucking missed him." I bit my lips together, tears welling in my eyes for the second time that morning. "I missed him. He hurt me, and I broke up with him. And I've missed him every single day since then."

Marley nodded, reaching out and rubbing her hand down my arm. "It's okay to feel things for him, Avory. And it's okay to forgive him."

"I can't forgive him." I was sniffling, my words barely a whisper. "He hurt me."

"And you hurt him." Marley turned back to making breakfast. "And you both hurt Cash. Your relationship was a fucking disaster from the beginning. You know that, right? You two were lying, sneaking around. Then you dragged his twin and your best friend into the mix. You two destroyed Cash without blinking an eye."

I hated thinking about what we'd asked of Cash, so it was something else I buried down very deep inside me. Crue told me that he did what he did with that girl to save me, to save his twin. And it wasn't that I didn't believe him, it was that it didn't make it better. It didn't make it all fade away.

Marley handed me a bagel. "Avory, you are as much at fault for your breakup as he is. You two made a mess, the both of you, together. You expected Cash's help, and you didn't care if it hurt him." Her words were true, and they made my heart ache. "Crue was trying to clean up something that both of you had a hand in. He was like a trapped animal, trying to save everyone he loved. He made a mistake, but so did you."

I let Marley's words rattle around in my brain, picking them apart as they settled in to stay. Crue was backed in a corner, and he did the best he could. I was at fault too. I was fine with using Cash when it suited me, but when it backfired, I jumped ship. I let Crue take all the blame, and I washed my hands of the whole situation. "I fucked up too." I buried my memories, and along with them, the reality of what actually happened all those years ago. "Holy shit. I fucked up too."

Marley nodded. "You fucked up too, Avory." She took a bite of her bagel, as if this wasn't a world-tilting conversation for me. "I don't know if you and Crue have a future, that isn't for me to say. But I do think it's high time you start seeing your past the way it really played out. He isn't the villain here, and deep down you know it."

I didn't see it then, I was a heartbroken teenager. But I wasn't that girl anymore.

Chapter Twenty-Six

Crue

Now

I wouldn't leave her alone, I couldn't. I was getting closer. I could feel it. At night, when I had her in my arms, she let her guard down. In the moonlight she didn't look at me like I was the bad guy, she looked at me like I was her hero. Like she had when we were kids. I'd never stopped loving Avory, and I would spend every day for the rest of my life trying to convince her to come back to me.

I was struggling like hell to distract myself. I'd already started a load of laundry and emptied the dishwasher. I wanted to send Avory more texts. I wanted to beg her to come back to the barn. I knew she hadn't left the compound because her car was still here, but she'd been gone for a couple of hours now. I wanted to know where she'd been.

"Hey, where've you been?" I picked Avory up, smiling when she wrapped her long legs around my waist. I loved her in her cheerleading skirt. It never failed to turn me all the way on.

She kissed my lips, tangling her fingers in my hair. "The game ran into overtime." She hopped down, climbing into the passenger seat of my truck. I walked around the hood, momentarily blinded by the headlights. I always picked up Avory after football games. It was our Friday night ritual. "But I'm all yours now." She made her bare shoulders dance. "My parents think I'm staying the night with one of the girls from my squad."

I rested my hand on her thigh as we left the stadium parking lot. "We got a whole night, baby spawn?" I curled my palm around her leg, sliding it toward her center.

She wiggled in her seat, my touch driving her crazy. "Yes." Her words came out like a whisper as my attention became more focused.

"Where to? Field? Back gate?" We had lots of places we ran away to be alone. But most of them meant we were hooking up in my truck or a blanket under the stars.

"Pool house." I raised my brows, but kept my eyes on the road. "I want to fall asleep next to you all cuddled up under the covers, and then I want to wake up to you without the fear of bugs in my hair." She leaned over the console, putting her lips against my ear. "I want you to make me scream, and then I want you to hold me all night long."

I nodded. "I want that too, baby. That sounds perfect."

I was so lost in my own head that I almost missed the sound of Avory's car door closing out front. Was she really going to leave without saying anything to me? I paused, unsure if I should play it cool and let her go, or if I should run outside and try like hell to stop her. In the end, I settled somewhere in the middle.

I walked out front, taking my time and refusing to let myself sprint. I stood on the porch, leaning my shoulder against the railing. She was sitting in her car, her hands on the steering wheel and her eyes on me. She looked like she had been crying, and her hair was a windblown mess. I crossed my arms over my chest, impatiently awaiting her next move. I didn't want to spook her by walking toward her. I felt like I was suddenly dealing with a scared deer. Where was the confident brat I was used to?

She rested her forehead on the steering wheel for a few moments before climbing out. She didn't come to me. Instead she stood in her open door. I made my way down the front walk, more than okay with meeting her in the middle of the standoff I didn't quite understand.

"I'm going home." She took a deep breath, then glanced down at her feet. "I need some space, Crue. I need to try to sort out some shit."

"I don't want you to leave." I'd been playing the asshole role and I'd been doing it well. But something about the tone of her voice, the uncertainty in her gaze. She was being honest, and I wanted to return the favor. "I don't want you to ever leave, baby."

Avory nodded, wiping at her cheeks. "I know you don't." She sniffled. "But I don't know how that makes me feel. And I need some time to figure it out."

Time? She needed time. I'd already given her way too much of that. "I've given you five years to figure it out." Would she ever love me again? Would she ever take me back? I never doubted that before. But standing here in my driveway, watching silent tears fall, I was suddenly unsure of everything.

"I didn't spend the last five years thinking about you, thinking about us." Her voice cracked. "I buried every single loving thing I felt about you down deep in a place where it couldn't hurt me anymore." She threw her hands up, letting her palm smack the top of her car. "And then bam, the floodgates opened and you're everywhere. Memories and texts and long nights tangled up in your sheets... Fuck. Crue. I spent so many years thinking you were the bad guy, the villain and, and, and—"

"And what, baby?" My scarred heart soared with hope.

"And I don't know anymore." She pushed her hair back from her face, her fingers sticking in the tangles. "I've got to go." She got behind the wheel, shutting her door and backing down the driveway before I could even process that she was leaving.

She'd shocked me with her raw emotions and her honest words. I stood frozen on my front porch until her car disappeared from my view. There was nothing I could do now but wait.

I'd made her see me. I'd made her remember our love.

And now I had to give her time to process it all.

Chapter Twenty-Seven

Avory

Now

Marley's blunt honesty shook me to my core. I left her house in a daze, walking all the way back to Crue's driveway. The sun was higher in the sky, its heat beaming down on me. I had every intention of getting in my car and not telling him I was going. But then I sat there so long that he came out to watch me.

He wasn't being an asshole. He wasn't cocky or demanding. He was silently strong. And that was the reason I told him what I did. That was the reason I gave him the only explanation I had. Every reason I had for dumping him, every reason I had for burying my feelings for him. They didn't make sense anymore.

My baby sister was right. Crue was right. It was my fault too. I was selfish, and I went along with every decision made. I was fine with Cash's sacrifices when they were benefiting me. I never spoke out. I never told him he should stop switching places with his twin. It'd never even crossed my mind. I was so hurt, so fucking mad at Crue for letting that girl blackmail him. Blackmail us. But what other option did he have? Cash would have been exposed. Our parents would have found out that we'd been lying to them for years. Crue was backed into a corner, and he did what he thought was best for everyone involved.

In the end, Crue learned from his brother: he sacrificed himself.

"Cash is a martyr. He's been picking Halen up off the floor every morning, helping her get dressed and get to school." Crue was sitting in the old chair by the back gate, and I was sitting on his lap.

"He's your martyr, too. He's been on like three dates in your place this month?"

Crue tugged playfully at my ponytail. "Can't have anyone finding out about us, then we wouldn't be able to sneak down here to make out." He kissed the side of my neck. "No more climbing into your window after your daddy goes to bed." He slipped his hand inside my shirt. "No more skinny dipping at the pool house under the stars."

"Well, we can't have that, can we?" I giggled when he tickled my ribs.

"No, baby, we can't have that." He sighed, leaning his head back. "Cash has always been better than the rest of us. It's who he is."

"Avory? Is everything okay?"

I smiled at the concern in Cash's voice when he answered the phone, dragging me away from the past. He was the kindest person I knew. "Yeah, I think it will be." I cleared my throat. "There's something I need to say to you. Can I come in?"

"Oh, sure, are you here?" Their front door opened, and Cash waved me inside. He was wearing his old ratty ball cap backward, his blond hair sticking out. I couldn't help but feel nostalgic looking at him.

I climbed out of my car, heading up their front walk. I'd left Crue's and immediately driven to Cash's. There were things, long overdue things, that I needed to say to the boy who used to be one of my best friends. If I was ever going to forgive Crue, I needed to forgive myself first. And that started here.

Cash held the door wide, closing it behind us. "Katie is still asleep, she was up feeling sick all night." He was speaking softly, not wanting to wake his pregnant wife. "You sure everything is all right? You don't look so great."

From anyone else, I'd be offended. But I knew Cash was honestly asking. I sighed, turning to face him as I shuffled my feet. "I'm sorry." His eyes narrowed, like he was confused. "I'm sorry for everything that happened when we were kids. I'm sorry for what we asked of you. I'm sorry that I was so damn selfish." I stepped closer to him, reaching for his hands. "I'm sorry that I let you put Crue and me first, over and over and over. I'm sorry."

He stared at me for a few moments, like he was letting my apology really sink in. They were words that I should have said a long time ago. "Come here." He pulled me forward, wrapping his arms around my neck. "I forgive you." He kissed the top of my head. "But, Avory, I'm a big boy. I made my own choices, and I made them out of love."

"We should've never put you in that position in the first place." I wrinkled my nose. "We were assholes."

He chuckled, letting me go. "He *was* an asshole, and you *were* a spoiled brat." The laughter left his eyes. "We aren't the same people we used to be, Avory. Being with Crue again doesn't mean you have to be the girl you were when you were seventeen."

"You know about Crue and me?" Not that there was a whole lot to know. But I supposed that we were even on speaking terms again warranted as newsworthy.

"Are you kidding? My twin is truly happy for the first time in five years. Who else could make that change in him?"

That felt like a lot of pressure, like an elephant sitting on my chest. "I shouldn't be in charge of anyone's happiness." Hell, I had a hard enough time conjuring my own.

"Maybe that came out wrong." Cash perched on the edge of his loveseat. "Crue is happy. He has a good life and he knows it. But he has never, not for one single day, stopped loving you, Avory. His life is incomplete without you."

Incomplete.

"What am I going to do when you're at UT? I'm so used to seeing you in the halls every day, my life is going to be incomplete." Crue was graduating in a matter of days, and my heart was already aching at the separation that was on its way.

"I'll still see you every day." He smirked. *"I'll still toss you in my truck to ride back roads."*

"What if it's not the same?" I was so utterly terrified that Crue graduating would make things change between us.

"It won't be the same, it'll be better. One step closer to us leaving this compound together." He moved his hands up my thighs. *I was straddling his lap in his parents' theater room.* *"And as long as I have you heart, your life will never be incomplete, baby."*

I took my heart from him. I ripped it out of his hands. That night, when I found him down by the back gate, he looked so destroyed. I knew he was hurting, but I was hurting too. And I chose me, like I always did back then.

Cash was right. We'd grown up. I might have been a brat when I was seventeen years old and in love, but that didn't mean I still was one. I was an adult now, and so was Crue. He'd been a bit of an ass over the last couple of weeks, but I was starting to wonder if that had been for my benefit and not his own. Either way, it was time to stop letting the past repeat itself.

Chapter Twenty-Eight

Avory

Now

After I apologized to Cash, I went back to my loft. Although I felt better, there was still a weight on my chest. On my heart. I was foolish enough to think that maybe taking that step, saying the words I should have said to Cash years ago would fix everything. Would give me the clarity I needed. But I was still confused, still torn. Memories kept assaulting me, stealing my breath and my ability to think clearly. The past was so vivid I felt everything I had back then. I could feel the love for Crue flowing through when I remembered all the nights he'd hold me, whispering sweet words into the dark sky. I could almost taste the lust, the way my body would respond to his every command. But it had all gone to shit, and I remembered that too. We'd hurt each other, and worse, we'd hurt Cash, the guy who'd martyred himself for his twin and me, and the guilt I felt over that wasn't a memory; it was new, raw, and extremely fresh.

I collapsed onto my bed, grabbed a pillow, and screamed into it.

I tossed the pillow that had been covering my mouth to the side, wrapping my arms around Crue as he rolled to the side and pulled me close. "Mmmmm."

"I've reduced you to sounds, not words. I like it."

I snuggled into his naked chest, sticky with drying sweat. "I formed words."

"You screamed my name. I'll also take that as a win for me."

My parents weren't home. They were in Austin for some event. But my sisters were, and screaming out my boyfriend's name in complete ecstasy seemed rude. So I'd grabbed a pillow and muffled my cries. "We need our own place. When are you going apartment hunting with Cash?"

I wasn't a fan of Crue and me not being at the same school next year, but I was beyond ready for him and Cash to have their own place. No more pillows over my face.

"Uh, we aren't." I turned over, meeting his wary gaze. "Cash got into school in Cali, they want him to play ball."

"Oh wow." Crue and Cash both played, but it was Cash's life, he loved it, and he was spectacular at it. "That's great for him, but what does that mean for you? Are you going to live here at the compound instead?"

He licked his lips. "I thought maybe I'd spend a year in the dorms, meet some new people. Maybe I'll join a frat and live in the house, I don't know. I've never really been without Cash, but it could be good for me, you know?"

"So Cash is moving across the country, you're going to move into a frat house and start letting sorority chicks blow you at parties, and I'll be here. On the compound. All alone."

Crue sat up, glaring down at me. "You think I'd do that to you? Jesus, Avory, I'm going to college, not getting a lobotomy. And alone? Are any of us ever alone on this damn compound?"

I knew I was being unreasonable, but I couldn't stop myself. Everything was changing and I was freaking the hell out. I wouldn't have Cash and Crue with me, and I didn't know what life looked like without them. I shrugged like I wasn't in the middle of a nervous breakdown. "Maybe moving away will restore your factory settings."

Crue shook his head, jaw clenched tight. I'd pissed him off. He got up, grabbing his jeans from the floor. "You're being a brat, and I don't have the fucking patience for it tonight." He pulled his shirt off my dresser. "Cash going to Cali is hard on me too, and you giving me shit isn't what I fucking need."

"Fine. Leave." I was shaking on the inside, but on the outside I had to give off the "I don't give a shit" vibe. I got out of bed, slipping on a shirt of his I'd long ago stolen. "You got what you came for anyway." So had I. I'd come so hard I had to put a fucking pillow over my face.

Crue scoffed, sitting halfway out of my window. "Your insecurities are showing, baby."

"Leave." I put steel behind that word when really I wanted to cry and beg him to stay.

He hopped out of my window and the moment he disappeared, I collapsed. The pain in my chest was so fucking real. Cash was leaving me, Crue was leaving me. They were both going to move on and I'd still be here. I couldn't live without Crue. I wouldn't survive the next year. What if he met someone better? Or what if he got drunk at a party and cheated on me? I couldn't control what I couldn't see. I was crying, heaving tears of frustration and trepidation.

"Come here, baby." I didn't hear Crue lift the window, but I felt him as he picked me up. *"It's all going to be okay, I promise."* He laid me back in my bed, holding me tight while I sobbed against his chest.

"I'm sorry I told you to go. I didn't mean it, I won't do it again."

He kissed my tears. "I love you more than anything in this whole fucking world and I'll never leave you." He pulled back, giving me a soft smile. *"No matter how hard you push."*

I tossed the pillow to the side, wiping the tears that memory had caused. We'd both lied. I'd pushed him away again, the night I broke up with him, and he'd let me. He didn't come after me, he didn't scoop me up off the ground and tell me everything was going to be okay. Not that time.

I thought it was because he knew he was in the wrong. I thought he was admitting guilt. But I could see now, that wasn't it. He needed *me* to be the one to hold him, to assure him we were all going to be all right. I didn't know how to be strong back then because I didn't have to be. I always had Cash and Crue at my side, being in charge and fixing what I broke. I was a spoiled brat, a child. But that wasn't me anymore.

I was better than the girl I used to be.

I was strong enough to be the one to pick us up this time.

Chapter Twenty-Nine

Crue

Now

I spent two days locked in my house. I wanted to reach out to Avory. I wanted to text her. I wanted to demand she tell me what she meant. I wanted to know if she forgave me. There was a spark of hope in my chest, the same one that had been there since she lied to me about breaking up with Colin by the back gate. I knew she had feelings for me. I knew being together the last few nights were bringing them back to life. But I didn't know what that meant for our future, and it was slowly killing me.

I was on the couch, watching baseball with a beer in my hand. I was trying to distract myself, trying like hell to go back to business as usual. I didn't want to let her moods affect my entire life, but like when we were kids, that was harder than hell.

"Bro. You're all twitchy and shit." Brody glanced over at me from his place on the floor in front of the flat screen. "I can hear your brain working overtime from here."

"Same." Jett was over too, posted up in my recliner. The early evening game was the perfect excuse for all the married and engaged spawn to run from their homes and into the old red barn.

"You want to talk about it?" Cash was sitting beside me, his position mirroring mine. We looked alike, had the same mannerisms. But that was where our similarities ended. I'd always loved my twin, but the older we got, the more I admired him. Respected the hell out of his kind soul.

I sighed. "It's Avory."

Jett chuckled. "Isn't it always? That girl has had you by the balls a long-ass time, broken up or not."

"Don't be a dick." Brody reached his hand back, slapping Jett's leg. "And don't act like Devin doesn't keep your balls in a mason jar in the damn kitchen."

"Avory came to see me yesterday." Cash's words were softly spoken, but we all heard him.

I turned to him, my eyes wide. "Yeah?"

"She came to apologize for everything that happened when we were kids." Cash's smile was small.

"Holy shit. Avory Connor said I'm sorry?" Jett raised his beer in the air, like he was saluting the room. "Anyone want to mark this day on the calendar?"

"Crue apologized the other night too." Cash punch me lightly on the leg. "But I forgave them both a long time ago."

"The brat *and* the asshole? Two unexpected apologies in a matter of days? Damn. You had a good week, C Money." Jett drained his beer, reaching into the ice bucket we'd sat on the coffee table for another.

"Is it impossible for you to not run your mouth? Do you have a medical condition?" Brody sat up, shaking his head at my younger brother.

Brody and Jett continued to rib each other and Cash spoke so only I could hear. "You and Avory aren't the same people you were back then. It's been five years, man." He paused, like he was trying to gather the right words. "You got her attention, you got her to let her guard down. Now stop trying to re-create the past, and start a new beginning."

***

The sun had set. Brody, Jett, and Cash had gone home to their families. I was still on the couch, unsure of my next move. Cash's advice resonated, and scared the shit out of me. New beginning. Starting over. I wanted to remind her of the guy she'd fallen for when she was fifteen, but had that really done anything other than get her in my bed? Did I make the right choice? Or did I simply lead her down a memory lane that ended in an epic crash and burn?

My cell vibrated in my pocket and I shifted on the couch to pull it out.

Avory: What are you wearing?

I almost couldn't believe my eyes. She'd texted me. Avory had initiated a conversation with me, and, basically, I was feeling giddy.

Crue: A smile.

Avory: You got plans tonight?

Crue: I've been sitting here for the last hour contemplating texting this girl I'm into.

Avory: And then she texted you first.

Crue: She did.

She was being flirty, and my heart was fucking soaring. Screw being seventeen again. I felt like a damn junior high boy with his first crush.

Avory: Meet me down by the back gate?

Crue: When?

Avory: Now.

Crue: On my way.

I hopped up, stepping into my shoes and leaving the house in mere seconds. I refused to run all the way to the back gate. I still had some cool points left and I intended to keep them. I was nervous and excited. But more than anything else, I was hopeful.

Chapter Thirty

Avory

Now

Pacing in the dark, making pass after pass in front of that old chair that had probably been down here since the beginning of time, I couldn't stand still if someone paid me ten million dollars. The night air was cool, the breeze chilling the slight sweat covering my skin. The moon was bright, low in the sky, and full. I'd gotten my ass handed to me by my younger sister, and I'd made an apology that I should have made more than five years ago. Damn, that was a lot, but at the same time, it was exactly what I needed.

Us against the world. That was the Devil's Spawn motto, and I'd lived it my whole life. But today, I truly felt those words down deep in my soul. I needed my family. I needed their advice, and I needed their input. I'd always thought it was hard to know who you were growing up on this compound constantly surrounded by other people and personalities. But I'd had it wrong because in the end I needed them to hold a mirror in front of my face to help me see exactly who I was.

I was Avory Connor. I'd fallen in love with a boy when I was fifteen years old. We made mistakes, we hurt each other, and we hurt the people close to us. But then we grew up.

I looked up and stopped my pacing at the sound of gravel under feet. I swallowed thickly, knowing Crue was close. I could almost feel him, his presence wrapping around me like a warm blanket. I waited, my heart racing.

And then he was there.

His hair was a mess, and his jeans were ripped. His boots untied and his shirt untucked. He didn't look quite like the boy I'd fallen for. Instead, he'd become the man I was still in love with.

"Hey." I waited as he came closer and closer, not stopping until he was close enough for me to smell his cologne. I breathed deep, letting it fill my lungs and give me strength.

His smile was tentative, like he was as nervous as I was. "Hey."

"Thanks for coming." I'd been a little afraid that after the way I left that morning he was going to tell me to fuck off. I was afraid that he'd grown tired of me pushing him away. But I should have known better.

He nodded, kicking at a small rock with the toe of his boot. "Always."

"There are some things that I need to say to you, and um, please just let me get them out."

He nodded again.

I took another deep breath, this time the scent of him so close making me a bit dizzy. "I'm sorry." It was like I was on a twelve-step program, changing the person I used to be and making amends on the way to becoming the person I wanted to be. "I was as much at fault for our demise as you were. You were backed into a corner, and I helped put you there. I see that now, I see it all. I forgive you. I forgive me. We were young, and we were ill-equipped to deal with the fallout from the thousands of lies we told." Lies we should have never told, lies we should have never asked our family to help keep. "I don't want to repeat the past. I want to start over."

I was done. I said my piece. I laid my cards out there, and now it was up to him whether he'd call or fold.

We stood in silence, staring at each other in the moonlight for so long that I almost thought Crue wasn't going to speak. But, thankfully, he cleared his throat and stepped even closer to me.

"I don't want to repeat the past either, but I refuse to forget it." He paused and my heart dropped to my feet. Had I misunderstood everything that was happening the last week? I'd apologized, but was it too little too late? Had I already pushed him over the edge? "I can't forget the way you looked dancing in the bed of my truck. I can't forget the way you fell apart in my arms the first time I made you come. The sound of your window in the middle of the night, the way you wore that tiny cheerleading skirt. I don't want to forget one single fucking moment of our life together, Avory. The good, the bad, the hurt, and the pleasure. All of it. It's mine, and I won't forget."

I gasped as he grabbed my hips, hauling me against him, kissing me deeply and stealing my breath. He cupped my jaw, pulling away a little so he could look in my eyes.

"I loved you then, I love you now, and I swear to you, baby, I will love you for the rest of my life."

"I love you too, Crue."

I cried as he kissed me, then he wiped my tears as he held me close.

Chapter Thirty-One

Crue

Now

It was Friday Family dinner, and Avory had walked by and let her hand brush against my ass. She winked, and jerked her head toward the pool house. I knew what my girl wanted, what she'd always wanted on nights like this. She wanted me to steal her away, to kiss her senseless in some closet deep inside the house with our parents none the wiser out on the porch.

I couldn't help but smirk as I moved to follow after her. It'd been a week since we met down by the back gate, where it'd all started when we were younger, and started again five years later. I'd like to say the intervening years didn't matter, but they did. Both of us needed to travel rough roads to get to where we were now. While so much about us was familiar, everything also felt brand new.

I'd been in her bed every night. We'd had coffee together on her balcony every morning. Sometimes we'd ride into work together. I couldn't get enough of holding her hand. I couldn't believe she was mine again.

"Where you going, bro?" Jett stepped into my path, blocking me from my girl and irritating me.

I chuckled. "We both know where I'm going." I shooed him with a wave of my hand. "Get out of my way."

He sighed. "Don't you think it's time for you two to stop hiding?"

He had a valid point, and it was something Avory and I had discussed several times over the last week. We were going to tell our parents, we had dinner plans with them on Sunday. We were going to sit them down and come clean about everything. Well. Not *everything.* She was fucking fifteen when we'd started hooking up. I wanted to be honest, not stupid.

I sighed. "We're telling them on Sunday." I shoved him out of my way. "But in the meantime, I'm going to have some fun." I walked past Jett and into the pool house.

I checked the small half bath, and when it was empty I continued on through the halls. I checked the bedrooms, the closets, and the other bathrooms. Then I got to the small pantry in the kitchen. I opened the door, shaking my head. "The smallest place? Really?"

Avory stepped back, making more space for me. "This way you have to hold me extra close."

"I planned on it." I picked her up, pinning her against the wall with her legs wrapped around my waist. I devoured her mouth, groaning as her tongue danced with mine.

Her hands went to the buttons on my jeans, making me laugh quietly. "Here, baby spawn?" My girl was insatiable, like she'd always been. And I fucking loved it.

"Crue."

The way she said my name, that one word telling me everything I needed to know. She wanted me, and I'd never deny her. I lifted her long dress, letting it gather around her hips. "Okay, baby, but you better come on my—"

"Holy shit, for the love of god."

Avory and I froze, her dad flooding the pantry with light from the kitchen. And this would be the moment I died. "Dad, um, I can explain."

"Nope." Uncle Dash held his hand up, stopping his daughter. "Crue, if you would kindly put your dick back in your pants, I'd like for the two of you to join me on the patio please."

Why wasn't he yelling at us? Was that the calm before the storm? Maybe he planned to grab a knife out of the block on the counter? Maybe I'd step onto the porch and he'd slit my throat, letting me bleed out in front of my poor parents.

"Yes, sir." I nodded, barely getting the words out of my throat without throwing up. He glared at me before turning away.

Avory spoke to his retreating back. "Okay, Daddy."

I waited until the door shut behind him before setting her on her feet. "Daddy? Really? While my dick is still inside you?"

"I'm sorry." She adjusted the strap of her dress. "I tend to revert back to the cuter five-year-old version of myself when I make him mad." She sighed. "It's going to be okay."

I opened the door, catching her smile once it wasn't pitch black. I raised an eyebrow. "Is it? Because your father just walked in on me fucking you in a closet." I shook my head. "I had actual nightmares of that happening when we were teenagers. And in my nightmares, he kills me."

Avory placed a kiss on my jaw. "He won't kill you."

She sounded sure, but I wasn't convinced. If I ever found a dude about to fuck my daughter, I'd commit murder.

I took Avory's hand in mine, and we walked out onto the porch together. When Uncle Dash saw us, he cupped his palms around his mouth. "Could all of you gather around please? I have something I need to say."

Well. Okay. He was going to make a public statement and then kill me. How exceptionally gangster of him.

Uncle Dash let out a deep exhale, then smiled. "I wanted to let all of you kids know, we're done." He made a motion like he was wiping his hands clean. "We pass the proverbial baton." He pointed at us. "Crue and Avory were our last loose ends, and it seems that's been settled."

My dad glanced from me to Uncle Dash. "What are you talking about? Have you been testing product with Marley and Jett again?"

"Luke. I just walked in on your son having sex with my daughter." Uncle Dash nodded somewhat manically. "And I can only assume, from their recklessness, they were *trying* to make us grandparents again."

We had *not* started trying for kids. We were simply that irresponsible. But I figured Avory's father wouldn't want to hear that, so I kept my mouth shut.

"You and her?" My dad looked confused. "You're hooking up with Avory?"

"Um, we're dating." Dating sounded shallow for what we were. "We're in love. We're um, together." I glanced over at Avory and she was hiding a smile behind her hand, finding humor in how uncomfortable I sounded. "We're, like, I don't know. She's mine. She's always been mine. We're end game. We're forever." I hadn't asked her to marry me, but I'd planned on it after we told our parents. I guess that part was done now. Maybe I'd ask her tonight after I made her come a few times.

"She's always been yours?" Uncle Dash narrowed his eyes. "Care to explain?"

"No. No we would not." Avory crossed her arms over her chest, glaring right back. "Didn't you just wash your hands of us?" Wow. My girl was *really* quick on her feet.

"Ah, yes, back to my point." Her father nodded again, like he was pleased she'd sassed him back on track. "All of you little spawn are paired up, in love, married, engaged, whatever. You've found your people. You're having babies, you're making babies." He paused to shoot a look my way. "And despite some road bumps, you're all decent humans. You work, you pay your own bills, you give to charity, and you take care of each other." He put his arm around his wife. "They say hindsight is twenty-twenty, and I used to wish I could go back in time and do better with you kids. Keep a closer eye. Be stricter. Dig deeper." He paused again. I assumed this time for dramatic flair. "But seeing you all standing here tonight, safe, happy, successful...I think either because of us or despite us, you kids turned out pretty fucking great."

I looked around the compound, seeing my family as a whole. Landry was a successful surgeon and she'd married a man who was utterly in love with her and their three boys. Beau and Halen had found their way back to each other, against some tough odds. They were married. They had a little girl and one on the way. Cash was a major league ball player, every little boy's dream come true. He had an amazing girl, and she was going to make him a father soon. Evie lost herself, and found love along the way. Nicky cherished her. We could all see it every time he looked at her. Jett and Devin were adorable, even though I'd never admit it out loud. He and Marley were saving the damn world, every fucking day. Talon was perfect for MVP, and we were all lucky he was part of our family. Emmie had gotten knocked up from a one-night stand, and turned out it was the best thing that could have ever happened to her, and Kase.

I'd broken Avory's heart while I was trying to save us. In the end, she'd forgiven me, and we'd forgiven ourselves. I'd never forget our past, I never wanted to. But from where I was standing, our future looked pretty fucking fantastic.

Epilogue

Beau

Uncle Dash had said it best. We were all paired up. All ten of us Devil's Spawn were happily in love, some of us with each other. Halen and I were married. We had two beautiful children. Both girls. Uncle Dash said I deserved girls after what I put his through. I didn't mind. Lennon and Irelyn were the best things that ever happened to me, other than their mother of course.

I'd been in love with Halen my whole life. I didn't remember a moment in time when she wasn't on my mind. I hurt her once, and I swore I would never do it again. And I wouldn't. I was beyond blessed. My girls were more than any one man deserved.

"Are you ready? I still need to fix my hair and Lennon just tried to put lipstick on Irelyn." Halen was standing in the doorway to my closet, her hair a wild mess and a baby on her hip. She looked gorgeous.

I finished tying my shoe, then stood and kissed my wife. "Come here, sweet girl." I took my youngest daughter from her arms and went in search of the other one. I thought Lennon took after her Aunt Landry, always a bit of mischief up her sleeve. She kept us on our toes: that was for sure.

Living this life of love and chaos on the Devil's Share compound continually reminded me that blood doesn't make a family. I didn't share DNA with one single person I'd grown up with, other than Uncle Smith, who, unlike everyone else who called him Uncle, was my real blood uncle. But not being related to any of the spawn didn't make me any less part of their world. I had amazing parents who gave me a home and the security I'd been denied as a young child. I had a big sister who gave me unconditional support and endless memories of laughter. I had brothers, younger sisters, and I had nieces and nephews. I had a girl by my side who loved me through every up and down life had to offer. And that girl? Well, she'd given me two more tiny hearts to worship and protect.

"Now, where is that big sister of yours?" I bounced Irelyn in my arms, turning the corner into Lennon's bedroom. I jumped across the room, interrupting what could have been a disaster. "You, my darling daughter, are going to make me go gray." I hooked an arm around her waist, pulling her off the little stool she was wobbling on. "What were you doing?"

She looked up at me, her eyes round and so very blue. "I want outside."

Her tiny voice melted my heart, and usually got her whatever she wanted. She communicated well, and only missed a few words here and there. "You were trying to climb out of your window?" I glanced from her to the window in question. "Why?"

Her tiny hands gripped the windowsill as she pulled herself up so she could see out of it. Her little toes anchored on the wall, giving her some extra purchase. "Wyatt's playing."

"You wanted to climb out of your window so you could go play with Wyatt?" She nodded and I took her hand, backing out of the room in search of my wife. "Sweets? We need to move."

***

Halen

Three minutes. That was the amount of peace and quiet I'd had to finish getting ready. I caught Beau's reflection in the bathroom mirror. He was holding Irelyn in his arm, and Lennon was clutching his hand. He never looked as sexy as he did when he was being a dad. I'd loved Beau Cole since the day I was born. Or at least that's how I saw it. And that love only grew as time marched on.

"What's up?" I smiled. "I'm almost ready."

Beau wiggled Lennon's hand, making her whole arm dance lightly. "This one was trying to climb out of her window so she could go play outside with Wyatt."

I bit my lips together to keep from laughing. Beau did not seem like he found that as funny as I did. "Lennon. It's dangerous to climb

things, and we don't use our windows to enter and exit this house."
Was rebellion in the soil here? Or maybe it was the water. Marley
would know. She had samples and data on both.

"We need to move." Beau's expression was so serious it broke
my resolve and a giggle escaped. "Sweets. This is serious. She was
using her window. Wyatt is older than her. And, and—"

"And she's a little girl who wants to go outside and play with her
cousins." I unplugged my curling iron, kneeled down, and opened
my arms for my oldest daughter. She ran to me and I picked her up,
raining kisses on her mischievous cheeks. "We still have years
before we need to start worrying about anything." I stood on my
tiptoes, kissing Beau as well. I headed off down the hall, the clock in
the kitchen telling me that we were going to be late if we didn't
leave now.

"Your dad probably put some juju on us." Beau followed me,
grabbing the diaper bag and hiking it up on his shoulder. "This is too
much karma for one person." I stepped out the front door, setting
Lennon down and laughing as she immediately flew off the porch
and ran to where Wyatt and Weston were playing. "See. She's in
love."

"She's three." Although she'd always favored Wyatt even
though Weston was closer to her age. "And my dad doesn't know
how to mess with anyone's juju. He's a retired rock star." If
anything, my dad would hire someone to do it, offer to pay them an
ungodly amount of money so he wouldn't have to lift a finger.

"We're installing more cameras, and motion sensor lights."

"Okay, babe." I took Irelyn from him, and he took my hand
helping me down the stairs.

"And alarms on all the windows."

I nodded, stepping into the field to help Landry gather the rest of
the little ones. "Whatever you say." I didn't need to remind him that
nothing would have kept us apart. No amount of sensors or lights
could stop two kids in love.

This compound was the backdrop of us, of our life together. Of
our love story. And now, we got to raise our little girls here. It
warmed my heart to see Lennon running through the tall grass, her
hands outstretched wide. She'd grow up on this playground, and
maybe she'd fall in love on it, maybe not. Either way, she'd be

surrounded by her family and by the people who would stand with her no matter what.

And having that, she was born lucky.

***

Landry

What a beautiful day. The sun was shining, the air was crisp, summer hadn't set all the way in yet, and I was grateful. Texas heat would have made it difficult to keep the boys in their little suits. Brody stepped out of the house, kissing my bare shoulder with Walker in his arms. "You ready, baby cakes?"

I sighed, nodding my head. I think we were all more than ready for this day, actually. "I'll get the bigger ones, you carry the baby?" Brody and I had three sons, and they were all clones of their father. Weston had his personality, whereas Wyatt reminded me of my brother. He was steadfast, protective. None of our children were calm though, and we argued over whose fault that was.

"Where's the diaper bag?"

"Crap, I left it inside. I'll go."

"I'll get it." He wrapped his arm around my waist, kissing my neck.

I smiled, leaning into his side, breathing in his sunshine smell. "Pack extra clothes for the boys. They're staying with my parents tonight."

Brody chuckled, the sound warming me all the way to my core. "I'm going to fuck you until you can't stand."

"Looking forward to it." I winked at him, laughing when he pulled his lower lip through his teeth, shaking his head.

"Such a bad, bad girl." He fused his mouth to mine, kissing me deeply until Walker grabbed a fistful of his hair and started squealing. "I love the fuck out of you."

"I love you too." I slapped his ass playfully. "Now go pack that diaper bag."

Brody deserved a night that was all about him, about us. I worked long hours at the hospital and he'd stepped up in the biggest way. It was hard to believe that a little over three years ago, I wasn't even sure who the father of my child was. Looking back on that time, I'm so proud of how far we've come together. Brody was the best man I have ever known. He was honest, light, kind, and loving. He was the most amazing father to our three boys, and an outstanding husband. He cherishes his family, all of us, and it's evident in his every action. I won the lottery the night I let him fuck me in a janitor's closet. How many people can say that?

***

Brody

I never thought I'd be this guy, the doting husband, and the dad. I always had kids climbing all over me, and I counted down the hours to bedtime so I could get their mother alone. Landry was everything I never knew I always wanted, and I was the luckiest fucker on the damn planet.

I sat Walker on the floor in his brothers' room they shared. They were so close in age, and honestly we sort of used Wyatt to keep an eye on Weston. Our middle child was a bit of a wild card. You never really knew what he was up to, and silence was always something to be concerned about. I grabbed pajamas and clothes for tomorrow, silently thanking the heavens above that the boys were staying with Jacks and B. I couldn't remember the last time I had Landry all to myself for a whole night.

Walker crawled over and started unpacking the bag. "Bro." I shoved the clothes back in, taking the diaper from his chubby hands. "Look, I know you're obsessed with your mom, but I am too. You're staying at Pop and BB's, it's happening whether you like it or not." He made another play for the diapers so I picked the bag up off the ground, zipping it closed. He squealed, balling his hands into tiny fists.

I scooped him up, shrugging. "You get her all the time. I'm asking for one night." I smacked a kiss on his cheek. "No hard feelings."

He grabbed a handful of my hair, drool dripping down onto my dress shirt. I gasped playfully, lifting him so I could blow on his tummy. "Why you so aggro? We both know she'll come get you first thing in the morning."

Landry was as obsessed with our boys as they were with her. She would act all elated when they were with her mom or a sitter, and then two seconds later we'd both start to miss them like crazy. I loved the life Landry and I had created here on the compound, and I loved our boys. And to think, it all started one crazy night after a show. I'd asked Landry if she wanted to have some fun, she said yes, and we hadn't stopped since that moment.

***

Cash

Katie and I took turns getting ready and feeding our boys. We'd learned to multitask like pros since having our twins. Bingham Luke and Hayes Paxton were still in their high chairs, cracker crumbs all over the place. They were wearing dress pants, but we'd opted to keep their tiny button-downs off until it was time to go.

When we'd found out Katie was carrying twins, we cried. At first it was tears of joy, and then it was tears of utter terror. My parents came over for dinner, laughing affectionately at our fear. My mom assured me that we'd be fine, simply because we didn't know any better. We didn't know what having one infant was like, so we would be too tired and blissed out to realize we were working doubly as hard.

It hadn't made a lot of sense when she said it, but once we brought the boys home, I understood. We didn't have anything else to compare it to, so to us, having two infants was normal. Twins being our normal didn't diminish the fact that my wife was a straight-up rock star though.

I helped a lot right after they were born, but by the time they were three months old, I was back out on the road. Major league ball waited for no one, breastfeeding wife at home or not. Luckily, Katie and I lived on the compound and there were always plenty of people around to help her out.

I glanced at my watch. "Katie, baby, we need to head out."

"Almost ready, the boys' shirts are on the counter."

I took one baby out at a time, cleaning them off and getting them the rest of the way dressed. We had maybe thirty minutes tops before one, or both of them, ruined their new clean shirts. They were close to crawling, and I knew that once they became mobile everything would change.

I'd tried to talk Katie into hiring a nanny but my mom had started bawling when she overheard. She wanted to be there for her grandsons. She said that was what retirement was all about. Well. She'd semi-retired. She was vetting replacements, tossing each application into the proverbial trashcan. When Katie needed help with the boys, my mom simply took them to the office with her. It was her company. She could damn well do what she pleased. Those were her exact words.

"They ready?" Katie came into the living room, looking like a daydream. Her dress was short, showing off her long legs. Her hair was down and wild, the way I liked it. She held her arms out, taking one of them from me.

I cupped her cheek in my hand, drawing her in for a kiss. "You look beautiful."

"Thank you." She smiled against my lips. "You look pretty good yourself."

I picked up the diaper bag, and we headed outside onto the front porch. The sun was shining and the compound was buzzing with activity. Today was going to be a really good day.

***

Katie

Our boys resembled their dad. They were blond with light-colored eyes. One was kind and mellow, and the other was bossy and wild. Cash's mom said that was the way with twins. They were polar opposites because they had to balance each other out. Bingham used soft hands and always let Hayes get his way. But no one could make Bingham giggle like his brother. It was so fun to watch the way they interacted with each other. It made me wonder what Cash and Crue looked like when they were tiny. Did they seem to have a secret language like my boys? Did they fall asleep looking at each other from across their nursery? Something told me they did. Cash loved his brother something fierce, and he'd gone through hell to give his twin the life he wanted.

I asked him once if he could go back and do things differently, would he? And he said no. He said that he'd have done it all over again if it meant that Crue and Avory got to fall in love. But that was Cash, so loyal, and so damn kind.

"Come here, boys, your daddy has an important job to do today." I was carrying Bingham, but I scooped Hayes out of Cash's arms.

He leaned forward, kissing them both on the head. "Hand one of them off, you don't need to try to keep them *both* calm through the ceremony." He straightened, kissing me before heading toward the ceremony site.

"I know Uncle Crue is your favorite daddy substitute, but he's getting married today so you're going to have to settle for Uncle Kase when he gets here." Our boys adored Crue. They would always smile and wiggle, raising their tiny fists when they saw him. I thought it was because they assumed it was Cash, but Cash and Crue swore it was because they had twin vibes and the babies recognized it.

Either way, Crue was a big help, and so was my baby brother.

"Hand me one of my grandsons." Luke stepped up beside me, taking Bingham and smacking kisses on his cheeks. "Hey, handsome, you boys clean up nice." He reached over and tickled Hayes's tummy. "And so do you, momma."

I laughed. "Thanks, it feels nice to wear something not covered in snot, slobber, or spit-up." My long flowing dress and freshly washed hair were going a long way to making me feel like a human again. "Your last one is getting married, how do you feel?"

Luke grinned, his eyes crinkling on the sides. "Peaceful and excited at the same time." He nodded, his gaze taking in the fields surrounding us. "The best is yet to come for all of you guys. Raising your kids here, together, watching them grow older and grow closer... It's special, and I'm lucky I get to stay a part of it."

I rested my head briefly on his shoulder, overcome with emotion. This place was special, and I was glad my boys would get to experience it.

When my father had banished me to the compound I now called home, I couldn't in my wildest dreams have predicted what was going to come of it. Cash did more than teach me how to live, he taught me how to love. And I would be eternally grateful for that short summer I spent within these gates, and the family it gave me.

***

Evie

"You ready to go little bird?" Nicky came up behind me, and put his palm on my still-flat stomach, smiling at me in the reflection of the mirror. "We're carpooling with Em and Kase, they'll be here in a few minutes."

I nodded, putting my hand over his. "Let's hope I don't throw up on the way to the compound."

I was ten weeks pregnant, we'd only found out a couple weeks ago. We'd been trying for a while, and we were beginning to think it wasn't going to happen for us, at least not the way we thought it would. And then, I'd started feeling sick in the mornings and getting up in the middle of the night to eat popcorn in the dark.

It took a solid week for Nicky to convince me to take a pregnancy test. I thought maybe I wasn't ovulating or maybe there was some other reason for my late period. When you've been trying for as long as we have, negative pregnancy tests are a bit of an emotional trigger and the thought of another disappointment was almost crippling. But it wasn't negative, not this time.

"We should tell your parents tonight, they'll be so happy." Nicky kissed the side of my neck. "I know you wanted to wait 'til you were twelve weeks, but I think it's time."

Nicky wasn't as cautious as I was. He wanted to shout our good news from the rooftops. I loved how excited he was, and I was trying really hard to let go of my fears and join him. "Okay, let's tell them."

Nicky and I lived in town, close to Emmie, Kase, and Luca. Nicky drove into work every day, running the Austin location of Revival Ink. Maykin and Bleu were handling the one in Dallas. Not only were they married, they worked together all day without killing each other, if you can believe that. I was sure that was a sight to see. The two of them arguing and then making up in between clients. Maykin was an artist, and she did custom work for Bleu's higher-end clients. She drew it and he tatted it.

I'd been working with RiffRaff for a few years, helping with their social media. And eventually I took over doing the same for

Revival Ink and MJ Botanicals. I worked from home a lot, which would be perfect when our baby was born.

I put my hand on my stomach one more time, already so in love.

***

Nicky

I watched Evie as the smile on her face and the hope in her eyes bloomed. I knew she was scared that something would happen to the baby, that this joy was too good to be true. Her doctor assured me that was normal for new mothers, and that all I could do was be there for her.

That part was easy. I'd be there for her until the end of time.

Evie had walked into my life and knocked me on my ass, and then she'd walked away. Then back in again, crashing into walls and destroying everything I thought I knew. She'd gone through so much to get to this good place we'd settled into. And I was lucky to be by her side.

My Uncle Waylon had retired and left Revival Ink to me. He'd built me a legacy and I hoped that one day I'd be able to pass it down to my kids. I didn't have a father growing up, but I knew what that love looked like thanks to my uncle.

When Evie and I decided to move to Austin, I was nervous. I was used to having her all to myself, living in this safe little bubble we'd created together. I always blamed her parents for the lengths she'd taken to hide who she was. I thought moving closer to the compound would be a trigger. But I was wrong. Being with her family again, having dinner and walking the caliche roads…it helped heal her even more.

Sure, it was chaotic and her parents were still pretty clueless, but the love that flowed here was unlike anything I'd ever witnessed before. There was a strength this place instilled in the kids who grew up here. And now, my child would get it experience it too.

***

Jett

Devin and I got married at the Austin courthouse. We didn't really invite anyone. Neither one of us cared about having a big wedding as much as we did about being husband and wife. Her parents were pissed off, and my mom cried. But eventually, everyone got over it. I knew Devin was the girl for me the first time she blew me off, and she'd kept me on my toes every day since then.

Watching the rest of the Spawn breed, she'd told me she wanted kids, so we'd have them because I lived for her happiness.

I'd been thinking a lot about it actually, and I came to the conclusion that I was going to be a fucking fantastic father. I'd spent the last twenty-odd years learning from everyone else's mistakes. My kid would NOT be able to pull the shit I did. I mean I built a tunnel under my father's feet. I grew marijuana on his land. I was going to keep a closer eye on my little spawn. And if I had a daughter? Forget about it. She wasn't going to be allowed to spend any time alone with Brody's boys. Cash's *maybe* because Cash would make sure they grew up kind and respectful. Brody and Landry's three blond tornados were trouble. Like recognized like.

I stepped onto the back porch, watching as Devin arranged a giant bouquet of fresh-cut flowers. You could take the girl off the working ranch, but you couldn't take working the ranch out of the girl. She wanted cows. We compromised with a giant garden.

"You ready, turtle? This thing can't really start without us." I pointed to the peonies in her hand. She looked so beautiful, her long dress blowing around her ankles with the breeze.

"Don't rush me. If this falls apart halfway down the aisle, I'll never forgive myself."

Crue and Avory were getting married. And all I could say was thank fuck. I couldn't watch another failed relationship attempt from that girl. We knew Crue was the only one for her, and so did she. But did that stop her from constantly bringing around all those Mr. Wrongs? Nope. We had tons of family photos with random strange dudes in them. Luckily Aunt Lex was a genius with editing. She always went back and erased their existence as soon as Avory dumped them.

And don't even get me started on my brother. I was pretty sure that guy hadn't laughed for five fucking years.

But now all that was behind them, and us. They forgave each other, and they moved on. It was admirable, and it was about time. I didn't love big weddings, but I was actually pretty excited about this one. Seeing my family happy made me happy.

I made my way over to Devin, my eyes drinking in the blue dress she was wearing. It was tight in all the right places and I was afraid I'd start drooling any second. "Let's dump the flowers with my mom and skip the ceremony." I wrapped my arms around her tiny waist while placing open-mouth kisses against her neck. "They won't miss us, and I want to make you come." I was excited for the wedding, but still perpetually horny for my wife.

She laughed, wiggling out of my arms. "We aren't missing that ceremony." Her smile turned wicked. "But we can skip that cocktail hour after."

I was so utterly in love with my girl.

***

Devin

I finished wrapping the bouquet with the pretty white ribbon I'd bought for the occasion. Jett was standing beside me, his shades in place. He was the epitome of cool, and he was all mine. When I fell for the cocky player in my sociology class, I got so much more than I bargained for. Jett gave me Marley, who was hands down my best friend. MJ Botanicals provided me with a career that challenged me every day. We built a gorgeous home, with a wall of windows in our bedroom and a gorgeous garden in the backyard.

But the best thing Jett had ever given me was the tiny baby growing inside me. We weren't planning on having kids for another few years, but it seemed like the universe had other plans. I'd only found out a couple days ago, and I hadn't told Jett yet.

I would though, tonight when we got home.

Or maybe when we snuck home during that cocktail hour. I wasn't worried about his reaction. I knew he'd be thrilled.

"Okay, done." I wrapped one hand around his arm, and we walked together around to the front of the house to the car that was waiting.

"Good. I'm already counting down the minutes until I can get you back here and out of that dress." Jett smacked my ass, making me squeal. "Fuck, I'm horny."

"You're always horny." We were riding over with Talon, Marley and Co. And when they came into view, I gasped. "Oh my goodness, is he wearing a tie?" I handed the flowers off to Jett and ran over to the toddler Talon was holding. "He's wearing a tie with a vintage baby Nirvana shirt, are you freaking kidding? I don't think I've ever seen anything so adorable." I took him from his father, snuggling him close. Tears were pricking the back of my eyes over how cute Co looked. Clearly, pregnancy hormones were kicking in quick.

"Are you crying?" Marley quirked one dark eyebrow. "Why are you crying?"

Ugh. Leave it to Marley to see everything and then not let you hide from it. "He's so tiny and perfect."

"He is perfect." Talon ruffled his son's hair.

"But not like cry-worthy." Jett put his hand on my shoulder, spinning his nephew and me to face him. "Turtle, what's wrong?"

I laughed, shaking my head. "Nothing is wrong, I swear. Everything is wonderful."

"Oh. You're pregnant." I whirled on Marley, a what-the-fuck look on my face. She simply shrugged. "Your boobs look massive and you're crying over my baby's t-shirt."

"Devin?" Jett sounded confused, and slightly hopeful.

Of course this was the way Jett would find out he was going to be a father, with both his girls here. I wasn't angry. In fact, it felt exactly right. I handed Co back to Talon, and then wrapped my arms around Jett's neck. I smiled up at him, more tears filling my eyes. "I'm pregnant."

He gave me that sexy smirk of his, palming my ass and pulling me tighter against him. "Good."

"Good?"

"I love making babies with you, and I know I'll love raising them with you too." He kissed my lips, dipping me backward. "So yes, good. Great. Perfect. Fuck yeah."

***

Marley

I didn't mean to announce Devin's pregnancy like I had. I figured Jett already knew and maybe they hadn't told the rest of us yet. But I was glad I got to be there, to see the look on my person's face when he found out that he was going to be a dad.

"I'm really happy for you." I patted Jett's hair when he rested his head on my shoulder. "You're going to be a great dad."

"I know." He sat up straight, smoothing his dark hair. "I had a good one growing up, and there's a pretty fantastic one who lives right across the street." His eyes narrowed. "And if you tell that husband of yours I said something nice about him, I'll deny it."

Jett and Talon had a comical relationship. They loved each other, but they loved hating each other just as much.

I looked to the field beside us, where Talon and Devin were walking with my son. They were each holding on to one of Co's tiny hands. He'd only learned to walk a few weeks ago, and the uneven ground was treacherous for his wobbly steps. But he refused to be carried. Talon said he was stubborn like his mother. I didn't think it was such a bad trait to know what you wanted though, so he could be bullheaded all he wanted.

I never thought I'd be a mother. I never really thought I'd ever be married either. My dreams weren't like other little girls'. I didn't fall asleep at night picturing wedding dresses and prince charming. I'd always been driven, ambitious. Instead of white picket fences, I'd conjured images of winning Nobel Prizes and curing cancer.

I guess I could say all my dreams had come true, even the ones I didn't know I had. Talon made my life sweeter, he gave it more heart. And Co, he was *everything*. I truly felt like I had it all.

***

Talon

I smiled, mouthing *I love you* to my wife who was watching me and our son with that soft look in her eye. Co and I were the only ones who could make her melt, and I took pride in that. She was saving our seats at the ceremony site, sitting with Jett. He and Marley were a package deal, and I'd come to terms with that years ago. They needed each other. They balanced each other out. One couldn't exist without the other because the world couldn't handle them separately. Jett may have been her soul mate, but I was her heart.

"You feeling okay?" Devin and I were walking with Co out in the field, trying to spend some of his toddler energy so he'd sit through the ceremony.

"A little emotional, and a little queasy. But other than that I feel pretty good." She smiled and then we both turned, heading back toward the family. "I only found out a couple days ago, so it's early."

"I'm sorry Marley spilled your secret." I knew she meant no harm by it. She had a *you see it, you say it* mentality. I loved her honesty, and her family valued it. But some people found it off-putting. Ask our employees.

Devin waved away my apology. "It was the perfect moment. It felt right to have y'all there."

"Yeah, I get it." Devin and I understood each other on another level, because no one else would ever be able to fathom married life with Jett and Marley. We shared our spouses. They didn't belong only to us. And we were okay with that because they were both more than worth it. "You going to tell the rest of the family? Luke and Lo?"

Devin scooped Co up into her arms, and I took her elbow, helping her over the small rocky patch of land. "Nah. We'll wait a few more weeks." We stayed in step, heading into the crowd of people waiting to watch Crue and Avory get married. Finally.

"Oh, what a beautiful little family." Some random lady stopped us, pinching Co's cheek. "Cherish these baby years, they grow up so fast." She sent us another smile, revealing lipstick on her teeth, and then walked away, speaking into one of those neck mic things.

Devin laughed, rubbing Co's red cheek. "You okay, kiddo? You gotta watch out for those amped-up caterers, they live on energy drinks and leftovers."

I put my hand on her back, helping her through the rows of chairs until she could sit beside Jett. "There you guys are, we lost you in the crowd." He took Co, holding him high in the air, wiggling him gently.

"The caterer stopped us. She wanted to tell us what a beautiful family we were." Devin rubbed her thumb lightly against Co's face. "Cheek pinches and all."

"It's going to be funny when you have a kid too, people never know who belongs with who when we're all out together." That wasn't the first time someone assumed Devin, Co, and I were a family, and I knew it wouldn't be the last.

"You know genetically, your baby will have dark hair like Jett." Marley's hand rested on my thigh. "Which means he'll look like us." She gestured between her and Jett. "The way Co looks like you two."

I wrapped my arm around my wife, pulling her close and kissing the tip of her nose. No, I didn't mind sharing her. Jett worked hard when they were young, making Marley's dreams come true. This compound was full of all kinds of dysfunction, absolutely, but it was also so fucking full of love.

***

Emmie

Kase pulled our large SUV into a parking spot, then rested his head against the seat. "One more wedding, and then we're all done, right?" Most of the Devil's Spawn hadn't cared to have a big ceremony. The majority of us had slipped off quietly and eloped. Uncle Luke said it wasn't fair that two of his sons had picked girls who wanted actual ceremonies. Uncle Dash said it was karma because Luke and Lo only had sons when Luke deserved at least one daughter.

The parents had a lot of inside jokes, a lot of memories and stories that we'd never understand. But so did we, so did the spawn. It's no wonder we grew up close. We saw our parents' connection to each other from the day we were born.

"Last wedding. Only gender reveals, baby showers, and kid birthday parties from here on out." Nicky clapped Kase on the shoulder then opened his door and helped Evie out.

Kase reached over the console, cupping my face in his hands. "You look beautiful, Ems."

"Thank you." I kissed his palm, more than okay with letting Nicky and Evie get Luca out of her car seat so I could steal a moment with my husband. "I love you."

He pulled me close, kissing my lips before getting out of the car, to come around to my side to open the door for me. "You know, we conceived Luca after a Mathews wedding."

I snorted. "Oh, I remember." I could still recall every moment of the first night we spent together. And I cherished every single second since then. Even when I was scared, even when we were both so unsure of our next move. Those early days of getting to know ourselves and each other: falling in love. They were invaluable.

Kase wrapped an arm around my waist, pulling me against his chiseled body. "You wanna leave this one early too?"

I nodded, licking my lips. "Yes, please."

"Hmmm, say it again, but with more of a whimper in your tone."

I straightened, putting my mouth against the shell of his ear. "Yes, please," I whimpered, breathing heavily as I squeezed his firm ass.

"You two want to leave now?" Nicky interrupted us, standing close with our daughter sleeping in his arms.

Kase nodded. "Sure would."

I took his hand in mine, dragging him forward. We couldn't miss this wedding. Like Kasen had said, it was the last one. We were all paired up, all in love and with the people we'd spend an eternity with.

***

Kasen

I cradled my baby girl in my arms, enjoying the soft sound of her breathing. She'd fallen asleep on the short car ride over, and she was still out cold on my shoulder. Her perfect little lips were squished together and she looked so damn cute in her pink tulle dress. I hoped she'd grow up and be a ballerina like her mom.

I loved watching Ems teach class. I loved seeing her in her tights most of all. She was the most beautifully graceful woman I'd ever known, and she was all mine.

We lived in town, but came back here for family dinners and to let Luca play with her large family. Ems didn't want our kids growing up here. She didn't want them running wild and getting into trouble. But I was starting to believe that there was something about this place, something almost magical. Luca didn't need to live on this land to hear its call. She was born a tiny spawn.

"I think we should stay with Katie next weekend after Cash goes back out on the road." Ems leaned over, kissing our daughter's soft lips and then kissing my jaw. "She's had help for the last week and it's going to be a shock to the system when he leaves again."

"Sure, we can do that." Katie and Ems were close. Hell, they were sisters. And staying at Katie's house made me nostalgic.

I'd fallen for Ems on this compound, at a weekend a lot like this one. There'd been music, and dancing. Her dress had blown in the breeze and I'd been instantly enamored. I could almost remember the pull in my gut, the way I *had* to talk to her. We'd spent a lot of her pregnancy hiding away at Katie's, getting to know each other, learning to take care of each other. I told Ems once that I thought we'd met for a reason, that we were supposed to create Luca. But now I knew it was more than that. We were supposed to love each other until the end of time.

Ems and Luca were my greatest adventure.

***

Avory

Today was my wedding day, and I couldn't wait to get it over with. My mother had made me spend the last two nights away from my fiancé. The first one was so I could have a special slumber party with my sisters, and the next was because it was bad luck to see the groom before the wedding. I think she was trying to torture me a little since she found out that Crue and I had snuck around this compound for a couple of years. She said I was too old to punish, but I think she found a way.

I missed Crue. Since we'd gotten back together, we hadn't spent one night apart. And being away from him for two was almost unbearable. I was addicted.

I figured we earned it, for what we'd gone through to get back to each other. We weren't the kids we were in the beginning, but that passion that ignited us was still very real. We'd always loved each other: we'd always craved that fire. But now it was like a low constant simmer instead of random explosions. Sometimes I wonder where we'd be now if we'd never broken up down by this back gate. Would we have stayed together the last five years, or would there have been another epic fight to separate us? We'd had some growing up to do, and I'm not entirely sure we could have accomplished it while clinging to each other.

There was no way of knowing for sure, and I guess it didn't really matter. We were in love back then, and we're in love now. We'll never lose the memories we had as teenagers; that was our beginning. But this, our ending? It was my favorite part.

"You ready? It's almost go—"

"Yes." I cut Halen off, taking my flowers from Devin. "Yes, let's go." I knew I sounded overeager, but I didn't care in the slightest.

"Okay." She rolled her eyes and then nudged Wyatt and Weston down the aisle. They were the ring bearers. We'd had a dress rehearsal last night and Weston had promptly lost the fake ring we'd given him. Turned out he tossed it into a pool at the bottom of a statue because he thought it was the same as throwing pennies into a well. Safe to say we didn't let him carry the real rings today. "Lennon, come on, sweet girl, you're next." Halen kissed her daughter's cheek and pointed down the aisle to where her little cousins were waiting.

Lennon took off running, giggling like a tiny fairy the whole way. She looked like she was going to launch herself at Wyatt, but Beau stepped in last minute and scooped her into his arms.

"For heaven's sake." Halen rolled her eyes as she started down the aisle toward her husband and oldest daughter. Marley stepped into place next, winking at me over her shoulder. And then it was my dad and me waiting for our turn.

"I know you're eager to get down that aisle, but can you spare a minute for your old man?" My father looked so handsome in his black suit, the tiny diamond-encrusted skull cufflinks sparling in the sun.

"Always." I smiled at him, adjusting his black bow tie.

"I should have paid more attention, Avory, to you and your sisters. I should have kept a closer eye on you three. I should have asked more questions."

"Dad, we—"

"Let me finish, sweetheart." He held his hand up, stopping me from telling him what I wanted to say. "There are a million things I should have done differently, but I'm glad I made mistakes." He smiled, his eyes moving past me to our large family seated and waiting. "Learn from them, baby girl, learn from the parents we were and do better when the time comes."

"You did good, Dad, you all did." I gestured behind me with my large bouquet. "We turned out pretty fucking great."

"You kids were always destined for greatness, and you would have gotten there with a lot less heartbreak if I'd have bolted your windows shut."

I couldn't help but giggle at what he was implying. I took a deep breath, putting my free hand on his shoulder. "That's how we learned to love each other. That's how we learned to take care of each other. Those open windows are what made us strong, Daddy." I smiled through my tears.

He hugged me close, both of us feeling so much emotion in that moment it was hard to speak. I understood where he was coming from, but I hoped my words helped ease his mind. I had wonderful parents, we all did. And it wasn't their fault it took us so long to realize that they would always have our back.

The music changed, letting us know it was our turn. My father let me go, his eyes bright. "You look beautiful, sweetheart." He kissed my cheek, rubbing a reassuring hand on my back. "But if you've changed your mind, scratch your nose."

I laughed, resting my head on his arm for a moment. "I haven't changed my mind." And I never would. Crue was my first love, and now he'd be my last.

***

Crue

I wasn't born in love with Avory Connor, but I sure as fuck would die that way. I'd lost her once, and I'd make sure that I never did it again. I wasn't the kid she fell for at this back gate, the one who demanded her compliance, and then yanked her into my arms. And she wasn't the girl who craved my dominance with a smirk on her lips. The people we were now were smarter than that, more empathic and compassionate. We didn't take each other or our love for granted because we knew how bleak the world was without it. Avory and I handled our separation in vastly different ways. She buried her pain and I wallowed in mine.

We forgave, we grew up. And so did our love for each other.

Standing here watching her come toward me, I clenched my jaw, trying like hell to hold in the tears threatening to fall. My girl walked down an aisle scattered with rose petals, holding a bouquet of flowers that were grown in the soil that had nurtured us. She was stunning, absolutely breathtaking. Her white gown hugged her body, the long silk train trailing behind her. Her long dark hair was down, the way I liked it best. She was smiling, her eyes on me.

I'd asked her to marry me in this exact spot. We'd gone on a midnight stroll and I'd stopped and gotten down on one knee. I proposed under the stars, right in front of that magical old chair. She'd said yes.

Today we were getting married here, and next week we'd start construction on our new house. The back gate was our spot, and now it always would be.

Uncle Dash placed Avory's hand in mine, glaring at me slightly as he stepped away. I couldn't blame him. I was the punk kid who snuck around with his underage daughter and then broken her heart. I'd glare at me too.

"You look beautiful, baby spawn." I squeezed her hands, my thumb rubbing over the diamond in her engagement ring. I'd put it on her finger only a couple months ago, but why wait to get married? I'd known I wanted to spend the rest of my life with her since I was sixteen years old.

She took a deep breath, squeezing my hands right back. "Let's do this."

I nodded, and we both turned toward Cash. He'd gotten ordained online because nothing else would feel as right as him blessing our marriage.

"Well, we all know why we're gathered here today." He grinned at us. "Love stories come in all shapes and sizes. I think this compound is living proof of that. Some people seem to be born in love, and some stumble into it when they least expect it.

"But I think we can all agree that a true love story never ends."

THE DEVIL'S SHARE FAMILY

Dash & Lexi Connor

Halen Connor Cole m. Beau Cole	Avory Connor Matthews m. Crue Matthews	Marley Connor Roberts m. Talon Roberts
Lennon Lex Cole Irelyn Connor Cole	Lyla Dash Matthews Margot Leigh Matthews	Caspian "Co" Owen Roberts Miles Jett Roberts

Beau and Halen's girls:

Since the kid's took Beau's last name, Halen wanted to add her last name to one of their children, and her mom's name to another. Lennon was a nod to both Halen's parents because they named her and her sisters after musicians.

Crue and Avory's girls:

Crue and Avory loved the name Lyla, and her middle name is for Avory's father, Dash. Crue picked the name Margot, because he liked the name and the old actress it reminded him of. Leigh is Avory's middle name.

Talon and Marley's boys:

Talon and Marley named their firstborn Caspian Owen because they wanted something timeless, and they wanted him to have Co as initials because of their shared fondness for Kurt Cobain. Both Talon and Marley loved the name Miles, and Miles Davis. As for the middle name, they lost a bet to Jett: if he guessed the baby's birth weight correctly he got to pick the middle name.

Smith & Dylan James

|

Evie James Barrens	Emmie James Cadence
m. Nick Barrens	m. Kasen Cadence
Cohen Waylon Barrens	Luca James Cadence
London May Barrens	Liam Mason Cadence

Nick and Evie's kids:

Nick and Evie chose Cohen for Leonard Cohen because they love his iconic "Hallelujah." They used Waylon as a middle name for Nicky's Uncle Waylon who helped raised him and founded Revival Ink. They thought London was a cool name, and her middle name, May, is for Evie's best friend Maykin.

Kasen and Emmie's kids:

While hanging out with the Spawn one night, Jett picked out Luca, and Kasen and Emmie loved it so it stuck. James is Kasen's sister Katie's middle name, which came from her birth father's favorite song "Rock On" by David Essex. Liam Mason is a nod to Kasen's father, the rock star Mason Cadence (Mason Maxwell).

Jackson & Bryan Cole

|

Landry Cole Frost   Beau Cole
m. Brody Frost   m. Halen Connor

| |

Jackson Wyatt Frost   Lennon Lex Cole
Weston Cole Frost   Irelyn Connor Cole
Walker Brody Frost

Brody and Landry's boys:

Brody and Landry's firstborn is named after Landry's father and Brody's father. Everyone calls him Wyatt. Brody and Landry's middle son is called Weston because that's Beau's middle name as well as the last name of the couple that was so nice to Landry in the hospital when she was pregnant with Wyatt. The youngest Frost is Walker because Brody and Landry needed another W, and Brody wanted his name somewhere in there, so Walker's middle name is his dad's first name.

Beau and Halen's girls:

Since the kid's took Beau's last name, Halen wanted to add her last name to one of their children, and her mom's name to another. Lennon was a nod to both Halen's parents because they named her and her sisters after musicians.

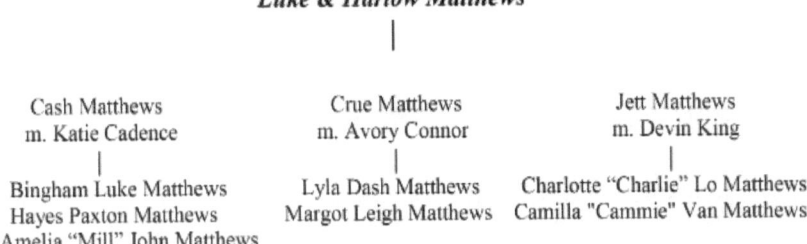

Luke & Harlow Matthews

Cash Matthews	Crue Matthews	Jett Matthews
m. Katie Cadence	m. Avory Connor	m. Devin King
Bingham Luke Matthews	Lyla Dash Matthews	Charlotte "Charlie" Lo Matthews
Hayes Paxton Matthews	Margot Leigh Matthews	Camilla "Cammie" Van Matthews
Amelia "Mill" John Matthews		

Cash and Katie's kids:

Cash and Katie's twins were named from their shared love of old school Texas country music. Bingham is Ryan Bingham, who sang the song that was playing the first time Cash saw Katie at a field party. Bingham's middle name is for Cash's father. Hayes is named for Hayes Carll, who sang one of Katie's favorite songs, the one that was playing in Cash's truck when he was touring her around the compound. Hayes's middle name Paxton is for Katie's uncle, the one who urged her to live a little. They named Amelia, Amelia so they could call her Mill, short for Millie, which was a character in the old baseball movie *Bull Durham*, one of Cash's favorites. John, her middle name, is for Katie's birth father who died the day she was born. Her much older brother Mason raised her as his own.

Crue and Avory's girls:

Crue and Avory loved the name Lyla, and her middle name is for Avory's father, Dash. Crue picked the name Margot, because he liked the name and the old actress it reminded him of. Leigh is Avory's middle name.

Jett and Devin's girls:

Jett and Devin liked the way their daughters' names sounded when they put them together. Charlie's middle name is for Jett's mom, who everyone calls Lo, and Cammie's middle name is for Jett's soul mate and business partner, Marley Van.

PLAYLIST

I'll Be There For You
-Bon Jovi

Reckoning
-Whiskey Myers

Why Can't You Love Me
-Wade Bowen

Them Shoes
-Patrick Sweany

My Name Is Human
-Highly Suspect

Fix You
-Coldplay

So Rich, So Pretty
-Mickey Avalon

Earned It
-The Weeknd

Mine
-Bazzi

If You Want Love
-NF

Hurt Somebody
-Dirt Drifters

ABOUT THE AUTHOR

L.P. lives in Austin, Texas with her husband, daughter, two rescue dogs, and one adopted cat. The first group of chickens met with a sad and unexpected death. They have been replaced. The dwarf goats are a story for another day, as are the ducks.

Writer, business owner, and office manager, L.P. says she loves to read as much as she loves to write. Reading a good book is her reward after writing one. In her spare time—ha!—she fosters puppies for a rescue organization based in Austin.

Connect with L.P.:

lpmaxa.wordpress.com

facebook.com/pages/LP-Maxa/1442560722667127

twitter.com/lpmaxa

instagram.com/lpmaxa

www.BOROUGHSPUBLISHINGGROUP.com

If you enjoyed this book, please write a review. Our authors appreciate the feedback, and it helps future readers find books they love. We welcome your comments and invite you to send them to info@boroughspublishinggroup.com. Follow us on Facebook, Twitter and Instagram, and be sure to sign up for our newsletter for surprises and new releases from your favorite authors.

Are you an aspiring writer? Check out www.boroughspublishinggroup.com/submit and see if we can help you make your dreams come true.

www.ingramcontent.com/pod-product-compliance
Lightning Source LLC
Chambersburg PA
CBHW051830170626
46807CB00003B/1105